Other Titles From Dev Love Press

Paradox

Devoted

(W)hole

Breath(e)

Ruth Madison

DEV LOVE PRESS

This is a work of fiction. Names, characters, places, and incidents either are the product of the author's imagination or are used fictitiously, and any resemblance to actual persons, living or dad, business establishments, events, or locals is entirely coincidental.

BREATH(E)
2nd Edition

A book by Dev Love Press, published by arrangement with the author

PRINTING HISTORY

Dev Love Press 2nd Edition/ October 2012
Create Space 1st Edition/January 2012

Visit our website at www.devlovepress.com

ISBN: 978-0-9858263-2-1

To my dear friends at paradevo.net:
without you, there would be no sequel.

This book is a sequel, but can be read on its own. Praise for the first book in this series, (W)hole:

"What a fantastic writer you are. You had me hooked by the end of the second paragraph...I've never been able to identify so completely with a female character until now."

"I read the book in 24 hours (on and off, obviously) and completely loved it. I'm so sad it isn't longer."

"I found much of it compelling. I was drawn to the main character Elizabeth and was very interested in her character development. It enabled me to understand sexual development in young women better. It was also an obvious pro-disability rights text which I very much appreciated. . . .The bottom line is your book made me think for sure. For that, I extend a very big thank you."

Chapter One

The reaction was not what Elizabeth had been hoping for. She uncurled her long legs and put her feet back down on the floor. She tried to sit up straight. If she looked like an adult, her parents might take her more seriously.

Susan placed a glass of wine down on a small round table beside the dark leather sofa. David cleared his throat and said, "It's just that Alcott College is so close to us, it would save a lot of money to have you live at home. That was one of the perks of choosing this school."

"But it's part of the college experience to live in a dorm." Elizabeth cringed as she heard a little bit of a whine creep out at the end. She had to behave like someone mature enough to live on her own. "I don't want to miss out," she added.

"I'd feel better if you were here," Susan said, not quite looking at Elizabeth, but rather at the fern behind her.

It was the opposite of what she would have said a year ago. Ever since Elizabeth became a teenager Susan had been trying to get her to be more outgoing and social. She had pushed her daughter to go out more, spend time with friends, stay out late even on school nights. That all changed when she found out about Elizabeth's boyfriend, Stewart.

Susan should have been delighted when Elizabeth finally started dating. She had tried many times to orchestrate meetings between Elizabeth and boys in her class. Stewart, being eight years older than her and in a wheelchair, was not what Susan had in mind.

"This was *his* idea," Susan muttered.

"No, mom, this is my idea. It's important for my development." Although Stewart really had inspired this realization in her. She had spent two weeks with him in California over the summer. The freedom from her parents had changed something inside her. The world looked different when it wasn't filtered through her mother's judgments. Elizabeth couldn't go back.

"You heard your father, dear; it doesn't make sense for you to live on campus. Soon enough you'll get a job and be out on your own. There's no rush."

David was looking at his wife with some surprise; he must have also noticed the sharp change in her approach to Elizabeth.

"Dad, please, can't we at least give it a try?"

"Let me think about it." He picked up Susan's wineglass and carried it toward the kitchen.

Elizabeth called after him, "I'm growing up; you'll have to face it soon." She flopped back in the stiff chair while her mother walked past.

She clicked on the TV and glanced at the empty living room, wondering for the thousandth time why her mother decorated their house like a high-class funeral home. Everything was in deep, rich tones. The furniture was heavy and oversized, thick carpets in colors like red wine and chocolate brown covered hardwood floors in nearly every room. There was a large framed print of Vermeer's *The Milkmaid* beside the mahogany wood cabinet that housed the small television. Elizabeth flicked through the channels, only half paying attention. This was all going to work out. She just needed to give it time for her dad to work her mom around to her point of view. He always did.

After watching a rerun of *Gilmore Girls*, she climbed the stairs and walked down the hall to her bedroom. This room was Elizabeth's safe space. The little closet had sheltered her during her darkest moments. Her boyfriend had never come here. He didn't know this corner of her heart. The stairs down the hallway acted as both a physical and an emotional barrier that she could choose to hide behind. She loved Stewart, but she wasn't sure she was ready for him to be completely part of her.

That night Susan came into her room. Elizabeth was startled by the door opening after she had already turned out the light. Her mother's shadowy form crossed the room and perched on the edge of the bed. "Were you a good girl today?" she said, touching Elizabeth's hair, the same straw color as her own. Elizabeth smiled. It was a tradition from when she was a child. Thinking back, it had started shortly after Susan miscarried the baby that would have been Elizabeth's little brother.

In those days Susan would often come into Elizabeth's room and lay with her in bed all night. Elizabeth never saw her actually sleep, but she would curl her body around the little girl, who would sleep pressed up against that place of loss.

"Good night, sweetheart," Susan said, squeezing her shoulder, and Elizabeth was grateful for this peaceful moment with her mother.

At breakfast Elizabeth squirmed on her chair. It was the same chair that had always been hers at the kitchen table, but it was too small. Its edges cut into her back in strange places, as she was taller than the chair expected her to be.

David scooped yogurt onto his cereal and said, "We've been talking about it, and your mother and I agree that it will be good for you to live on campus. It will transition you into living independently."

Elizabeth dropped her spoon with a clatter, ignoring Susan cringing, and grinned. "Really? Thanks, Daddy," she said. She could always count on her dad to convince her mom. In private he somehow always worked Susan around to Elizabeth's point of view.

"Just a few rules," Susan added.

"Like what?"

"You keep in contact, come home often, make sure we know what you're up to."

"I can live with that."

Elizabeth could see the start of a new life where she set the parameters. College was all new people and she could start fresh. She could create a persona. Maybe she would even pick a new name to go by. The possibilities were all right there in front of her. She was going to become grown-up Elizabeth. Responsible, ambitious, perfectly-put-together Elizabeth. No one there would know about her insecurities, her odd anti-social tendencies built over years of hiding the secret of her sexuality.

"I'll take you shopping this afternoon for all the things you'll need," Susan said. Elizabeth noticed that her mother already had a list printed out of college essentials for new students.

That evening she sat cross-legged on her bed and wondered which things she would take with her to college. She wouldn't need most of the things in her room and she would need things that she didn't have. A bathrobe perhaps. A laundry basket. A trash can. A bulletin board would be a very collegey thing to have. She would bring a copy of the magazine with her photograph in it, her first piece of professional pride. But she wouldn't want her new friends to see the teddy bear sitting on the corner of her bureau. Maybe she would buy a photo frame and put a picture of her parents in it. A chill, like freezer crystals, settled around her heart. She felt as though she were asking to travel to a new planet.

The weekend before orientation, Elizabeth and her dad packed. Susan organized everything in carefully packed and labeled boxes and David and Elizabeth carried them to the car. The boy who lived next door came out and leaned his chin on the fence between their yards.

"What are you doing?" he said as Elizabeth walked by with an ironing board in her arms. She stopped and put it down, wiping sweat from her forehead with the back of her hand. "I'm moving to college," she told him.

"Wow! That's cool."

"Yeah," she agreed, "It is."

"Are you going across the country?"

"No, I'm going to school in the city."

"I would go across the country. I'd go to school in Florida. Or California. Or Hawaii." His voice got louder with each possible location. "Some place warm," he concluded.

"It's pretty warm today," Elizabeth pointed out. Of course, it was also muggy and humid.

The boy made a dismissive gesture. "If I had a reason to go somewhere nice, I would take it."

Elizabeth laughed. "I like Boston," she said.

"You can have it," he declared and wandered away to pick up a basketball and toss it at the birch tree in his yard.

When Elizabeth saw her new room at the dorm she couldn't help wondering if her mother had somehow orchestrated this too. Sometimes she thought there was no end to her mother's reach. This idea was silly, though; all the freshman singles were tiny. It was narrow, with a bed so close to the desk that a chair wouldn't fit. And on the subject of chairs, Elizabeth could see immediately that Stewart would not be able to get his wheelchair through the door.

The next weekend he tried anyway. Elizabeth waited for him outside, sitting on the stairs in the sunlight. It was the end of August and the air was so muggy and warm that it was hard to believe that it would ever be cold, even though the bitter winter was likely to begin in a month.

She saw Stewart approaching from the other side of campus. He rolled smoothly and deftly along the path in a sleek red wheelchair. He wore a t-shirt and his thick, muscular arms were visible, the motion of wheeling showing them off perfectly. The edge of a tattoo peeked out from under one sleeve. His built upper body was a stark contrast to his compact legs, tucked beneath him. Even the bulk of cargo pants couldn't hide how thin they were. A peaceful satisfaction wrapped around Elizabeth's stomach. He was the man of her teenage fantasies and it still surprised her that he was in her life at all.

He smiled his disarming grin as he pulled up in front of her. She leaned down and kissed his lips, then turned to lead him into the old, brick building. "I'm telling you," she said, "You're not going to fit."

"Hey, I want to welcome you to your new home and celebrate the start of your independence with you," he insisted, following behind. Elizabeth unlocked her door and pushed it open. She looked at Stewart and he laughed. He bumped his wheels against the door frame. "Yeah," he said, "you're right, this is never going to happen."

"Let me show you the student center," Elizabeth said. She locked up again and led him across the sidewalk to a building smelling like floor wax and marinara sauce.

There were other students walking back and forth, but no one in the lounge area. Elizabeth flopped down onto a hard, green sofa. Stewart parked in front of her and she stretched her long legs up on his lap. Even after knowing Stewart for almost a year, she was still fascinated by his legs. Sometimes they seemed to move on their own and it was hard to believe that he really was paralyzed. He looked like he was just a man sitting down; it was amazing to think that he couldn't stand up. Other times she saw his hopelessly thin legs, the knobby knees that threatened to poke through his pants and she knew those legs could never support weight.

"So here you are," he said, "a college student. What do you think?"

She brought her gaze back up to his hazel eyes. "It's great. I was so ready for this."

She didn't have his full attention. There were people walking by and his gaze kept darting to the side, a reflex cocky half-smile appearing for each girl. He was getting plenty of looks back too. He was far too good looking. Elizabeth wondered why everything had not solved itself as soon as Stewart declared himself okay with her physical attraction to disability, her "devoteeism," as he called it. Wasn't that her "happily ever after" moment?

"Oh," Stewart said, taking one of her feet in his hands, slipping her shoe off, and massaging her flesh with his powerful thumbs, "by the way, Robert said to say hi."

"He did?" Even though her foot was relaxing under Stewart's touch, the rest of her tensed at the mention of Stewart's roommate.

"Sure. He likes you. Why do you look so surprised?"

"He doesn't like me." She and Robert didn't have a great history. He took Stewart's aunt's instruction to watch out for Stewart extremely seriously.

"Of course he does."

Elizabeth could barely concentrate on her own thoughts as Stewart kneaded her foot with his incredibly strong hands. Was it worth telling Stewart what Robert had said? *"I would love to pretend that it's totally normal for a beautiful young girl to throw herself at a paraplegic man, but we both know that it's not usual."* The truth was out between Elizabeth and Stewart, but not with Robert. At least, not that she knew of. A horrible thought entered her mind. What if Stewart had told his friend? What if Robert knew about her fetish? She couldn't ever look him in the eye again if she thought he knew that paralysis turned her on.

"You didn't tell Robert about me, did you?" she burst out.

"What about you?"

"You know." Elizabeth widened her eyes and cocked her head in a way she hoped was meaningful. She didn't want to bring up this highly personal topic by name in the student center at her brand-new school. She was supposed to be reinventing herself, not spreading a rumor and giving herself a reputation as a sexual freak.

"No," Stewart said, "I didn't tell him anything. Why are you suddenly so tense about Robert? He might have a stick up his ass, but he's harmless." Stewart switched to her other foot.

"It's not sudden," Elizabeth said, "We're just not fond of each other."

"He's a good friend. I would like for my girlfriend and my roommate to get along."

"We're, you know, civil."

"That's the best I'm going to get?"

Elizabeth crossed her arms and looked to the side, staring at the ugly green fabric of the sofa under her. She tried not to see the gorgeous lines of Stewart's wheelchair and his beautifully still body. "He said something to me last year," she whispered.

Stewart frowned. "Something about what?"

"You and me. Why I'm with you. He said it was up to him to protect you." Elizabeth pinched the flesh of one hand. "You know, from perverts."

"It sounds like Robert's forgotten that his job is imaginary. I'll talk to him about it."

"No, don't do that! You'll embarrass me. I just want to forget it happened."

"Obviously it's not forgotten."

"Please, Stewart, just let's move forward."

"Okay, but are you still coming over next weekend?"

"Of course. I'm not going to let him get to me."

After watching Stewart wheel off towards the T station, Elizabeth walked back to her dorm and smiled at the girl across the hall from her room, who was taping decorations to her door. Elizabeth had met her briefly a few nights ago when everyone on the floor had an ice breaker game with the R.A. The neighbor's name was Cassie and, according to the game, she was from New York.

"Was that your brother?" Cassie asked, trying to hold a construction paper "S" against her door and get a piece of tape at the same time. Elizabeth walked over and took the roll of tape, helping to attach the letters.

"Who?" she said.

"That guy I saw here earlier."

Elizabeth was tempted to make Cassie sweat, to force her to identify Stewart by his wheelchair, but she didn't. "Oh, Stewart? No, he's my boyfriend."

Cassie looked satisfyingly startled. "Oh," she said, forgetting to pick up the next paper letter, "good for you. Was he, I mean, did he get hurt while you were together?"

"No, he was in a wheelchair when I met him." Elizabeth surprised herself with how much easier it was to talk about than it used to be. For most of her life she had been unable to utter the word "wheelchair" and now it flowed off her tongue. She found that she enjoyed the surprise that registered in people's faces. She had fun shocking them by challenging their expectation of what life must be like for someone in a wheelchair.

"Well," Cassie said, "that's really good of you."

Elizabeth didn't know what to say to that assumption. She wasn't an especially good person, she was someone dating a man she had chemistry with, nothing saintly about that. "He's a good guy," Elizabeth said, wanting to go on a rant about how physically disabled people were still good partners and good lovers, but she was trapped by her own shyness.

"Oh yeah," Cassie said, "I'm sure he is. But still. That's got to be tough."

"Not really." Elizabeth shrugged. Cassie didn't look convinced. To change the subject, Elizabeth said, "What do you think I should put on my door?"

"We can go shopping at the Dollar Tree," Cassie said. "I'll help you pick out some stuff. This is fun, huh? It's almost like sleep-away camp."

Elizabeth had never been to sleep away camp. Each time her mother tried to sign her up, Elizabeth got so nervous and upset about it that she became violently ill days before she was supposed to go. She just nodded at Cassie, hoping that this would form a bond of some kind. Elizabeth was going to need friends here and she had never tried to make friends on her own. The ones she already had were girls she had been going to school with since she was six and at that age they had bonded over a shared favorite crayon color. It had always been easier to just keep hanging out with the girls she already knew than to find new friends. New people meant new risk of exposing her secret. Though she had known for most of her life that she was different from other people in her desires, she had not told anyone about it until she met Stewart last year. Even then she had kept him from finding out for many months.

Over the next week Elizabeth started her classes. She was startled by how much open time there was. Four classes instead of the eight she'd had during high school, and their times were spread out across the day. She could read books at noon, study in bed, and start her days without an alarm clock. There was always something interesting happening each time she walked out her door. At the end of the week there was a fair for all the campus clubs. They set up tents and the students could learn about each one. There were so many people and new things to do. Instead of a gym class with a choice between volleyball and basketball, Elizabeth could now pick fencing or dance or tai chi, or nothing. The freedom was everything she had hoped for.

She raved about it to Stewart that weekend at his dorm. He laughed at her enthusiasm.

"I already know what I'm going to major in," she announced.

"Let me guess," Stewart said, nodding toward the camera she had brought with her.

"Photojournalism," Elizabeth said, sitting up straight on the armrest of his sofa. "Doesn't that sound awesome and professional?"

"What do your parents think about it?"

Elizabeth sank down onto the seat of the sofa. "I can make some choices on my own, you know."

"Really?"

"Okay, I haven't told them yet. But they know this is what I love."

"I get the impression your mom is going to expect to have some input."

"I'll convince her."

Stewart laughed. "Like you convinced her of me?"

Elizabeth shrugged. "She's learning to tolerate you," she said. She put her hands on his knees and leaned over his legs to kiss him. "You know what?" Elizabeth said.

"What?"

"It bothers me that you don't let me be in the room when you're getting ready for bed. And I'm not going to leave anymore. Whatever it is that you need to do, you can do in front of me."

Stewart coughed and picked up her wrists to push her back onto the sofa. "Look," he said, his voice tight, "the truth is, I need some time alone, you know, to decompress from the day."

Elizabeth frowned. She pulled her knees into her chest. "What?" she said. She felt a chill spreading through her stomach as she tried to understand what he was telling her. "Are you saying that you've been using your disability as an excuse to keep your distance from me?"

"That's not exactly how I'd put it."

"Oh? How would you put it? We hardly get to see each other as it is." Panic was changing the pitch of her voice. She tried to force it back down, to keep the fear from overtaking her.

"I'm doing my best, Elizabeth. I'm not good at this coupled-up stuff."

Elizabeth stood up and felt the blood rushing from her head. "I'm going to go," she said. Stewart tried to grab her hand, but she shook him off and went for the stairwell so he wouldn't follow her. Why did it startle her so much to find out that all the nights they had spent together, when she was out in the hallway waiting for him to finish his routine, that it was a lie? She had put so much trust in Stewart, allowed him to be the guardian of her emotions. She felt a little betrayed.

Chapter Two

The seat rattled as the subway train chugged away from Stewart's school. Elizabeth curled her fingers around the hard red plastic and felt the underside of the seat cutting across the insides of her hands. A half-crushed Dunkin Donuts cup rolled by against the direction of the train. Every time the doors whooshed open, Elizabeth smelled the stale air of each underground station.

At her stop she swung out onto the platform, taking the steps two at a time. The sting of the cold night air was a welcome change and she breathed deeply as she strode back to campus. Elizabeth was glad Cassie's door was closed and she could go right into her broom closet of a room and close the door behind her, knowing that no one would bother her.

She sat on the bed with her back against the wall and her feet on her desk chair. The mattress was stiff underneath her. What was going on with Stewart and her? He felt distant still and she was getting tired of it. There was a whole new world opening up for her and he seemed to be pulling her down. She ran her fingers into her hair, squeezed her head, and closed her eyes. This was crazy. Stewart was her dream come true. He was her fantasy come to life and delivered straight into her arms.

Yet, she had been squashing some doubts. Every once in a while she found that she couldn't really picture their future together. They didn't have very much in common. His being a paraplegic and her being attracted to paraplegics wasn't all they had, was it?

Elizabeth leaned over and grabbed her cell phone out of her school bag, looking at the time. It wasn't too late. She called Amy. In the last several months Amy had separated herself from Elizabeth's other friends and they had become much closer. It was Amy who had skipped school to comfort her when Stewart and she went through a rough patch. It was Amy who was the first person Elizabeth ever told about being a devotee.

While the phone rang, Elizabeth pulled her hair out of its ponytail and shook her head. She balanced the phone against her shoulder and pulled open the blinds of her one window, watching people stumble by, looking for parties.

"Hey!" Amy's bright voice chimed on the other end of the phone. Elizabeth flopped back on her bed and smiled at her friend's familiar voice. "What's up?" Amy said.

"How is beauty school?" Elizabeth said. Lying back as she was, she could see that her ceiling light was starting to flicker. Who was she supposed to contact about that?

"Eh. Not as much fun as you'd think. Seriously, though, it's 11:00 on a Friday night, what's wrong?"

"Nothing urgent. I'm just not as sure about me and Stewart as I used to be."

There was a pause almost long enough for Elizabeth to wonder if they'd been disconnected. Then Amy said, "I've told you before; you two are really different and it seems like you're only with him for that one part, for the physical stuff."

Elizabeth rolled over onto her stomach, propped on her elbows. "I don't think that's true! I like him a lot as a person. But I do feel something lacking, like I can't ever quite relax and be myself around him. It's just that he came into my life in such an amazing way and I think that has to mean something. What are the odds of me finding someone so physically perfect for me?"

"Maybe his purpose in your life was to help guide you to acceptance of yourself and you've done that now.

Just because we love someone doesn't mean we are meant to be with them forever."

"But how can I walk away from this when it's so hard to find decent guys in wheelchairs?" Elizabeth held the phone with one hand and with the other she picked up strands of her hair and lifted then dropped them.

"Do you hear yourself? Your number one reason to be with him is you're afraid you won't find someone else. That's not fair to him or to you."

Elizabeth sighed. "You do have a point there."

Stewart called her on Saturday. She had kept meaning to call him all day, to say something, but each time she picked up her cell phone she didn't know what to say. He felt like a stranger in some ways. Despite how close they had become, she was suddenly aware of how much she didn't know about him.

"Are you really that pissed?" he said.

"I don't know," Elizabeth said. She picked at the skin on her arm. What was she feeling? She really wasn't sure.

"I'm coming over."

"I have homework to do."

But Stewart had already hung up. Twenty minutes later he was knocking. When she swung open the door, Elizabeth found Cassie trying unsuccessfully to get out of her room. Stewart's wheelchair was blocking the entire hall and Cassie was standing in her open doorway with her hands on her hips.

Stewart gave Cassie one of his gorgeous grins and backed up with his hands directly on top of his tires, since there wasn't enough space to grab the rails on the sides of the wheels. He backed up to the front door and Elizabeth followed, keeping her eyes past his shoulder to make sure he didn't run into anyone. They went to the same place in the common hall again.

"What's going on?" Stewart said.

Elizabeth looked at him, taking in his deep black hair and the dramatic contrast of his hazel eyes, his strong face that almost looked like it had been chiseled from stone by a very patient craftsman. She twisted her arms together, unsure of what she wanted to say. "The thing is, I was young when we got together and I've never been with anyone else."

She paused, looking down to the sandwich shop on the lower level. Was she really going to do this? She remembered how incredible she felt when Stewart first asked her to dance a year ago. Even as she thought back to that moment, it didn't feel like she was even thinking of herself; it was less like a memory and more like a movie she had watched and enjoyed, then returned. Looking back to Stewart, who was silently waiting with a neutral expression on his face, she continued, "I'm not the same person I was when we met. And this is a new experience, college. I want to do it all, you know?"

"I see." He pressed his lips together, then smiled and said, "I care about you, Elizabeth, but you're right, you are young and you should have the chance to meet different people and find yourself." He leaned forward, resting his elbows on his legs, and took one of her hands in his. "I'm actually thinking of moving back to California."

"You are? When were you going to tell me?"

"I was going to talk to you about it. I haven't had a chance."

"Right." She knew he must have been thinking about this ever since their two weeks in California that summer. He couldn't find time to mention it until now?

"I have an unfinished life there," Stewart continued. "Whatever happens, though, I want you to be part of it."

Elizabeth smiled. "Me too," she said.

"So you're breaking up with me?"

She paused to consider one more time, then nodded.

"I understand," he said. He squeezed her hand in his strong grip and then kissed it. "We'll talk again soon." He quickly readjusted his body in the chair and pushed off on his wheel rims.

After he left, she waited for the pain, but it never came. She was remarkably at peace with no longer being a girlfriend. As she walked back to her dorm room, she felt lighter. Small leaves were drifting down from the trees and the sunlight gleamed off the windows of the buildings she walked between. It was beautiful. A sensation of peace rose through her stomach and lungs and into a smile. All the possibilities in the world were open in front of her.

As she opened her door, she saw the message light flashing on her phone. She knew it must be Susan; no one else ever called her on the dorm phone. Elizabeth pressed the button and her mother's voice filled the small room, twittering on about all the things Elizabeth should remember to do: take vitamins, change her sheets, apply for a new library card.

Elizabeth sighed as the message continued on. What was she going to tell her mother about breaking up with Stewart after all the trouble she had gone through to date him in the first place? The last thing Elizabeth wanted was an "I told you so" from her mother. And what would happen when Elizabeth met someone else and had to introduce her parents to a second man in a wheelchair? It was difficult enough the first time. If she did it again there would be no way to avoid some uncomfortable truths.

A few months ago when Elizabeth first discovered there was a word for her desires, she had made the decision not to tell her parents about it. She reasoned that it would be selfish of her to force them to discuss fetish and sexuality when they weren't prepared to deal with that. It had felt incredible to say it out loud with Stewart and with Amy, but she didn't want to upset her parents with it.

Now she started to wonder if she would be able to manage to keep it from them forever. Could she continue to date disabled men without having them draw the connection? Could she continue to bring disabled men home and just not say anything, pretend that it was a totally normal thing to do? She decided to avoid telling her parents about the breakup just yet, even though she talked to them on the phone almost every day and was going home for fall break in just a couple of weeks.

As the days went by, it did start to feel a little strange not to be talking to Stewart as much. Sometimes she reached for her phone to call him when something amusing happened, but then she didn't. She wasn't sure what friendship with him looked like. They had only ever dated.

In the evenings as she fell asleep alone she missed him. She could hear a life going on outside her room that she didn't feel quite connected to. The girl whose room was on her left played music late at night that came into Elizabeth's room, muffled. There were footsteps going by all the time. Cassie was a connection, though. If Cassie's door was open, Elizabeth often went over there and sat on her bed talking in the afternoons.

Cassie was taking classes in special education, but seemed to have a very different mindset about disability than Elizabeth did. Elizabeth was careful not to say anything when her new friend's opinions sounded condescending and patronizing. She didn't want to isolate new people, though she tried to throw in references to disability as a civil rights issue whenever the opportunity came up.

"What does your boyfriend think about cuts for special education budgets?" Cassie asked one afternoon. She was sitting at her desk while Elizabeth occupied the bed. The room was an exact replica of Elizabeth's room, except reversed, and just as small. There were some double rooms and roommates in this building and it was just luck of the draw that had given them each singles their freshman year.

"I don't think he really thinks about it."

"Is he on Medicare?"

"No. He's a year away from graduating with a teaching certificate and a degree in physics." She didn't think he was on Medicare, anyway. She wasn't actually sure. She had never asked Stewart about those aspects of his life. It sounded better for arguing with Cassie if he wasn't. "And, actually," she added, "we broke up."

Cassie was a lot more surprised by his college education than by the breakup. Her verdict was, "It's noble and all, but you don't want to tie yourself to that kind of future."

Now was her moment. Now was when Elizabeth should say that actually she did want to tie herself to that kind of future and would do so again if she could. It was the perfect opening to be an out-of-the-closet dev, to tell Cassie that a paralyzed man was exactly what she was looking for. She looked over at Cassie's face. Her friend's mouth was scrunched to the side in a questioning expression. Elizabeth admired her short red hair and porcelain-doll face. The dev life felt very far away. Cassie turned back to her computer, found something to laugh at on Facebook. Elizabeth's moment passed. She could think of no way to tell her new friend about her sexuality without sounding like the worst kind of freak and someone Cassie would never relate to.

That night, feeling alone in her world, she called Stewart.

"Hey there," he said. "How are you?"

She shrugged even though he was three thousand miles away by now and couldn't see her. "Okay," she said.

"That doesn't sound great. Come on now, it's me. You can talk to me."

"Yeah," Elizabeth said. She smiled. It was true. There was no one she trusted like Stewart. He understood her in a way she wasn't sure anyone else ever would. "I was just feeling alone."

"Anyone you want me to beat up?"

Elizabeth laughed. "That won't be necessary."

"Well, let me know."

"I will. How is California?"

He paused and she heard a cheer in the background. "Remarkably unchanged," he said. "Sorry about the noise. I'm at Jeff's bar and there's a game on."

"I should go and visit you some time."

"You should."

Elizabeth stretched out on her bed and sighed. "Thanks for talking," she said.

"Any time," Stewart answered and she could picture the cute half-smile on his face. Affection flooded through her. Stewart made a good friend and Elizabeth felt grateful that he was in her life. She slept well that night.

"College is awesome," Elizabeth told her dad when he picked her up to take her home for fall break.

As she snapped on her seat belt he looked over at her and said, "That's good to hear. What's awesome about it?"

Words like "awesome" coming from David made Elizabeth want to giggle. She watched him navigating the Boston streets out into the suburbs. He had shaggy brown hair, a short beard, and an easy smile. Elizabeth looked nothing like him. Few people would guess they were related. He was a simple man, always easily fascinated by whatever was in front of him.

"I like having control over my schedule and over my life," Elizabeth answered.

"Well, don't go wild. You know your mom and I are nearby and we can help with anything you need."

"Dad, honestly, can you see me going wild?"

David smiled. "No, sweetheart." He parked the car and Elizabeth got out, hopping up the steps ahead of him.

"How is everything?" Susan said as soon as Elizabeth dropped her bag on the floor next to the front door.

"Good."

"That's it?" Susan raised an eyebrow at her.

"That's it," Elizabeth said with a forced shrug. She still hadn't told her parents about the breakup with Stewart and she didn't know when she would find a good time to mention it. Last year she had alienated and upset her parents in order to date him and this year she was letting him go.

"Well, don't leave your bag there in the middle of the floor," Susan said.

Elizabeth picked it up and carried it to her room. Pushing open the door slowly, she found the room was mostly the same, just slightly Susanified. The bookshelf had been reorganized by book size and some removed to make room for a picture and a vase. The wall color was the same, but all the taped up pictures were gone and a couple of framed prints covered the old tape marks. The teddy bear on her bureau was gone and a piece of pottery was in its place. Everything about the room felt just the slightest bit straighter; sharpened corners where there had been fuzzy edges. It reflected more Susan's vision of what she thought Elizabeth was rather than what she really was.

Although Elizabeth wasn't sure what she really was. The only thing she knew was that she was in flux. Despite her plan to improve herself, to instantly transform into a better version of herself, she found reality a bit different from her visions. She had not become the grown-up Elizabeth she had planned, and yet there was a new person emerging slowly from the cocoon of her past. She just couldn't yet tell who this new person was.

When she came downstairs Susan said, "I think it's time you learned to drive."

"Right now?" She motioned towards the downstairs bathroom, wanting to go in and see if Susan had turned her darkroom back into a regular bathroom.

"You're living on your own and I just think it's a bit ridiculous that you don't know how to drive."

Elizabeth sighed. "Okay. Let's go." Once Susan had an idea in her mind, there was no point trying to do anything else. Everyone in the house had to follow her schedule and her plan. It was easier not to fight it.

Susan brushed her hands down her pencil skirt and led the way out the door. Her car was in the driveway and Elizabeth got into the driver's seat.

"Put on your seat belt."

"I've done that part before, Mom."

"Don't give me attitude. The brake is the bigger pedal on the left; hold that down with your right foot."

"Why my right foot?"

"You drive with one foot. That's how it's done. Don't be difficult. Now, keep your foot on the pedal while you turn the key. Keep turning until the car comes on. Okay, that's fine. Very, very gently take your foot off the brake. Now move your foot until you feel the edge of the gas pedal. Gently! Don't touch it yet." Susan pressed her hands on the dash in front of her.

Elizabeth began to move the car forward in jerky motions of a tiny bit of gas and sudden full-on brake.

"Don't lean in so close," Susan said. "You're gripping the wheel too tight."

Elizabeth tried to sit back, but she was too tense. Every muscle in her back was on alert and her mother's constant, sharp voice was not helping.

"You're not listening to me, Elizabeth."

"I'm trying to."

There was a reason Elizabeth had never learned to drive.

"You're going to be a terrible driver if you don't learn to relax," Susan said. "We should stop now."

"Fine with me." Elizabeth turned the car off, tossed the keys in Susan's lap, and shoved the door open.

At dinner that night Elizabeth didn't volunteer any information, still trying to avoid telling them about Stewart's leaving for California. Her dad asked about each of her classes in turn and she gave a brief summary of what she had learned so far. Susan was quiet and it seemed to Elizabeth that there was something she wanted to say and was showing as much restraint as she was capable of. The clink of forks against the edges of plates seemed to be tapping out a rhythm. An S.O.S., perhaps.

Elizabeth decided to bring up the juiciest gossip on campus. "A girl got expelled last week."

"Already?"

"She was a sophomore, not a freshman, but yeah, they found out she was selling naked pictures of herself. Can you believe they would kick someone out for that?"

"Yes," Susan said, "how horrible. I don't know about this school if someone like that was accepted."

"I'm afraid it's the times, dear," David said. "Not the school's fault. There's a lot more of this moral depravity going on."

"I don't see what's so horrible about it," Elizabeth said. She speared three green beans on her fork.

"Elizabeth!"

"Not that I'm going to do it or anything. It just seems like her own business how she makes money."

"She is part of our society, and as a community, what we all do matters," Susan said. "I hope you've signed up for a civics class."

"Maybe next semester," Elizabeth muttered.

After dinner, while Elizabeth helped to clear dishes from the table, Susan said in a tone that sounded like she was trying hard to sound casual, "And how is Stewart?"

"He's fine, I'm sure."

"Oh?"

Elizabeth finished putting the plate she was holding in the sink and looked at her mother. "I decided I needed to try out a variety of . . . experiences."

The relief in Susan's eyes was evident. In fact, it looked triumphant. "Thank God that's out of your system," she said, closing the dishwasher door. Out of her system? Elizabeth had a sinking feeling in her stomach as she realized that this was never going to end. She and her mother would continue to butt heads over this issue forever without ever having an honest conversation about it. Elizabeth would just keep showing up with disabled men and not saying anything about it and Susan would silently boil.

"Look, I know you have trouble meeting men, so I'm going to help," Susan said. She dried her hands on a clean dishcloth and folded it again, laying it neatly on the counter.

"Please don't do that."

"It's not your fault that you're young and inexperienced. I can set you up with some people. You'll see what a normal relationship can be like."

Normal. What a terrible word. Why couldn't her mother see that a relationship with Stewart was not abnormal? Two people trying to get along and be in love, what was so not-normal about that? The temptation right now was huge to tell her mother the truth, to say that one paralyzed boyfriend was not the end of this journey. Elizabeth bit her lip. She was going to be good; she was not going to upset her mother. She would be heading back to school in a couple of hours; she could keep her mouth shut.

"I know just the fellow."

"I'll think about it, Mom."

"Don't dismiss me; you don't want to miss opportunities to meet someone special."

No, she didn't. Her mother knew how to play on that fear. All of her life, her mother always convinced her to do things by saying that she could meet the love of her life. She shouldn't skip gym class, what if she met someone special there? Even though Elizabeth was on to her tactics, it still worked. The logic was too clear, how could she not take advantage of every opportunity? Why shut down the possibility of love with someone unexpected?

Since the dishes were done, Elizabeth finally went to check out the hallway bathroom. As she expected, when she opened the door it looked like an ordinary bathroom. She flicked the switch and plain white light illuminated a room decorated in white and black with touches of ivory. The tub was gleaming white with a shower curtain depicting twisting black flowers across it, and a large mirror in a thick ivory-colored frame hung over the sink. It was unrecognizable. Elizabeth sat down on the edge of the tub as she used to do and leaned her head against the tile side of the shower.

Her memories of the hours spent in this room seemed false. The room made her think that she had imagined it all. There used to be a red bulb in the light fixture. There used to be plastic trays laid end to end on the floor. There used to be a tarp covering the sink counter and a string tied from the shower curtain rod across to the vanity light.

Elizabeth was being erased from this house. Now that she had declared her independence from her mother, there would be no going back. Susan was making sure of that.

Chapter Three

"I'm going to give you a makeover," Amy said. She was perched on Elizabeth's desk and Elizabeth was sitting cross-legged on her bed.

Elizabeth laughed. "Right now?"

"Sure," Amy said, "It will be good practice for my mid-terms."

"Okay, sounds fun."

"How was fall break?"

"My parents are driving me crazy."

"Mine too. They think a career in beauty isn't good enough for our family."

"That sucks. Mine still don't know why I went out with Stewart."

Amy picked up Elizabeth's hair and ran her fingers through it. "Have you told Becky or Maureen?"

"No. You didn't say anything, did you?"

"No, sweetie. It's your sexuality; it's up to you who you talk to about it." She pulled a makeup kit out of her over-night bag and spread tiny containers of color over Elizabeth's desk.

Amy dabbed a brush in powder and buffed it on Elizabeth's face. "Still no idea where it came from?" she said.

"No. You've known me all my life, can you think of anything?"

Amy thought for a few moments, the makeup brush hovering unmoving in front of Elizabeth's face. "No," she agreed. "Nothing stands out."

"Exactly." Elizabeth sighed. "I wish I knew, but I don't think there is a reason. I really don't."

"So," Amy said, "Are you making new friends?"

"I'm terrible at making friends. And I don't know how to be authentic with people when I have this thing.

Like, I don't want to be secretive about it anymore, but I also can't just burst right out with it either. And it's scary to think about how potential new friends might take it."

"Yeah, I would wait. Get to know people and tell them later if you must. Do you really have to at all?"

"I guess not. But how much friendship can I really have with someone if I can never tell her who my crushes are and what I hope for in a relationship? I don't have it in me to go back to being secretive. If I see a hot guy in a movie or something, I want to be able to mention it!"

"You'll figure it out. Close your eyes."

Elizabeth obeyed and felt the light flutter of Amy's makeup brush over her lids. "Okay," Amy said. "Where's there a mirror around here?"

"Bathroom down the hall."

"Oh. Well, come on." Amy dragged her down the hall to the bathroom and they both looked at Elizabeth's face in the mirror.

"I look nice," Elizabeth said.

"You do." Amy grinned and threw her arm around Elizabeth's shoulders. "I should take get a picture of you for my portfolio."

Walking back to her room, Elizabeth said, "My mom is setting me up with people. I just want to say to her, unless they can't walk, don't bother."

"You really think you're not ever going to date an able-bodied guy? Shouldn't you at least give it a chance?"

"It would be a waste of time."

"You're sure?"

Elizabeth looked down at her fingers. "No. Not really. I'm not sure of anything at all."

"Let me set you up with some super-hot guy, and if you don't have sparks, then you'll be sure."

"Deal."

That night at the dining hall, Amy had her eyes open. She looked past Elizabeth's shoulder a lot, scoping out the possible boys to set Elizabeth up with. "Got one," she said.

"Already?" Elizabeth said.

"He likes you." Amy tilted her head slightly in the direction she wanted Elizabeth to look. Elizabeth turned her head and saw a handsome upper classman looking at her. Quickly, she spun her head back and opened her eyes wide at Amy.

"He is cute," she acknowledged. Elizabeth wanted to give him a chance; she didn't want to be chained to this thing.

Amy smiled at the boy in a friendly way and it was only a few minutes before he was standing next to their table. Up close he had a nice smile, but his canine teeth stuck out further than the others. His hair was brown and slightly shiny with gel. He was definitely cute, but Elizabeth's body was cold, completely neutral, no reaction. Elizabeth ignored that. People said that chemistry could grow, so she would give it a chance. Always before she had experienced immediate attraction, an instant warmth in her body. That must not be the only way.

"I'm Patrick," he said, looking at her. He didn't see Amy's self-satisfied smirk.

"I'm Elizabeth."

"You're new?"

She nodded. "Freshman."

"Ah, so who do you have for Writing 104?"

"Hansen."

"Cool. I've heard good things about him. Say, there's a Halloween party at my dorm on Saturday, you want to come?"

"Sure."

"Cool; it's Stanley Hall at 8:00. I'll see you there."

As Patrick walked away, Elizabeth thought about last year's Halloween when she was just starting to get to know Stewart. So much had changed in one year. It was interesting to think how you could go from not knowing someone at all to knowing them deeply over the course of months. Suddenly she wanted to talk to Stewart, to hear his reassuring voice.

"Good start," Amy said. "I gotta get home. You're excited, right? Going to enjoy the party?"

Elizabeth smiled. "Yeah, I'll enjoy it." In fact, she could already feel it. Maybe this really would work. Maybe if she just found the right guy, the devoteeism would loosen its grip on her.

Sometimes it felt completely gone. In those moments Elizabeth wondered if she were ever able to find another disabled man to date, could she sustain it? Could she really handle it day in and day out? She told herself that if they could handle the disability, so could she. People did it all the time. Of course, they didn't have a choice and she did.

During those times she could almost look at paralyzed guys the way normal people did. She would wonder why she ever thought she needed all that trouble in her life. She could pick an average life at any time. Would she be satisfied with it forever? For certain periods of time yes, but the desire always seemed to return. In the past, anyway. Maybe this time would be different. Maybe Patrick would be the key.

"Do you want to come too?" Elizabeth asked.

Amy shook her head. "Can't. I'm going out with this kid."

"What kid?"

"He's nobody, really, just someone to test out. It's not a big deal."

"Maybe Cassie will go with me."

"Are you afraid to be alone with Patrick?" Amy said, arching an eyebrow.

"I guess, maybe a little."

"You're going to be great. There's no pressure, okay? Just see if you like it."

They went back to Elizabeth's room and Amy packed up her things. "Call me after the party!" Amy said before she left.

Having been to a college Halloween party last year, this time Elizabeth knew she should pick a sexy costume. She couldn't resist trying to be clever, though. She took the bus to the Goodwill and put together an Amy Pond outfit of tights, corduroy mini skirt, tank top, plaid shirt open on top, and a scarf.

When she showed up at the party, she found that only half the people had any costume on at all and of those, most came from plastic bags at the Halloween super store. There were a lot of people and Elizabeth wasn't sure how to find Patrick. She wandered for several minutes, trying not to bump into people before she found him. He was wearing a Green Lantern costume.

"*Dr. Who*, right?" he said when he saw her.

"Yeah." Elizabeth smiled. She was impressed he recognized her costume.

Patrick introduced her around. The people at this party seemed younger than the ones at the party at Stewart's school last year. Now that she was a college student, other college students didn't seem so cool and special.

She did start to miss Stewart. She remembered his costume dressing up as his friend, the way he came through the doorway on crutches and surprised her with his height. She had felt so proud to be Stewart's date. She didn't feel that with Patrick. He was fine and he was cute, but there was nothing in her that wanted to show him off.

Elizabeth took stock of her feelings every few minutes. So far, so good. She felt sexy. It was a little weird when Patrick touched her, held her hand. It felt slightly wrong and the thought of kissing him was like the thought of kissing a woman. But that was silly.

She didn't know any of his friends and quickly she began to feel bored. She wandered away from Patrick and pulled a digital camera out of her pocket. The camera made her feel like she had a purpose in being there; it allowed her to fit in. She got unlikely groups of people in costume together and took their pictures. The party was starting to be fun.

Patrick brought her a drink and touched her arm. She smiled at him and listened to him tell her about his plans for the future: exploring the world, building new technology, being an important part in something big. At the end of the night she felt slightly relieved to leave him. But that must be just nerves, totally normal.

"Can I see you again?" Patrick said as she prepared to leave.

"Um, sure," Elizabeth answered.

The next time she spoke to her mother on the phone Susan asked, "Did you do anything fun for Halloween?"

"Actually, yeah, I did. I got invited to a party."

"By a boy?"

"Yes, by a boy." She smiled at the upbeat tone her mother's voice suddenly took.

"Oh sweetheart, I'm so proud of you."

Not proud of her work or anything school related. No, Elizabeth's mother was proud of her for getting a date.

"See, I told you it wasn't hard," Susan said.

"I've had dates before."

"Yes, well, that was different."

"It was?"

"You know very well it was. Now you see you don't need to seek out charity cases. Nice boys will be happy to take you out."

Stewart looked like a charity case to her? He was still the most gorgeous man Elizabeth had ever seen. Sometimes Elizabeth wondered what the world looked like through someone else's eyes. She was curious to know what other people saw when they looked at Stewart. It mystified her that anyone could see something other than a confident, sexy, charming man.

Elizabeth and Patrick went to a campus screening of a movie the next week. It was nice enough, but it felt a little bit like playing house. The date didn't feel real in some way. Elizabeth was just following a script, doing what she thought she should. They started walking around campus holding hands after that, but Elizabeth was hesitant to take it any further and Patrick didn't push.

The next week there was a lot of excitement on campus over some gay rights laws in the media. This was the first election Elizabeth was voting in and she was pretty excited about it even though she didn't follow politics very much. She realized that for several people on campus this was also their first election. Maybe that's why they were taking these issues very seriously.

Outside the library there was a table with pamphlets and a number of students holding signs against giving rights to gay people. *Warning: God Will Judge You. Children Need a Mom and a Dad. Homo Rights Are Not Civil Rights.*

As they walked past, Patrick waved cheerily at the protestors, and gave a thumbs up. Elizabeth pursed her lips. "You agree with them?" she said, trying to keep her voice steady.

"I don't have a problem with gay people," Patrick said, "I just think they should keep it to themselves, you know? I don't want to know what they do in their bedrooms."

"But maybe they don't want to know what we do in ours, either."

"What?" The look he gave her was so uncomprehending that Elizabeth said, "Never mind."

She didn't know why she saw herself in them. But if Patrick was so closed off on this subject, how could he ever handle her sexual difference? Just because she was with him didn't mean it was gone and she was now normal. It was still in her. If he found out would he turn on her? Call her disgusting? She tucked her hands further into her coat pockets. He was never going to find out. Besides, it did feel almost gone and she started to wonder why she had thought disability was so important in her life. It was just for fun. She didn't really need it.

The next weekend, Elizabeth went home and brought several loads of laundry with her. She was stuffing her clothes into the washer when Susan came down to the basement and said, "Are you separating colors and whites?"

"Yes."

"And delicates from studier things?"

"Yes." This was a lie. Elizabeth didn't have much that could be classified as delicates, and it seemed a waste to do a small load with only those. She wasn't going to say that to her mother, though. Susan wanted everything to be done a particular way.

"So," Susan said, "are you still seeing that boy from Halloween?"

Elizabeth closed the lid of the washer and turned the dial to start the cycle. She looked at Susan. "Yeah," she said, "I am."

"Pretty serious, eh?"

"Sure." It made her mother happy and she was going to do what she could to make it work. This was a new chapter in her life.

She was so determined that this was a fresh start, that night she located her box of devotee materials to get rid of it all. She had books, movies, and a notebook full of pictures that she had taken or gathered over the years. Maybe these tokens of devness were holding her back from fully investing in Patrick. They might be like talismans, containing all the dev power within them, not in Elizabeth herself.

With the books and movies packed firmly in the box, lid closed, Elizabeth asked her father to drive her to the Goodwill. As she left the donation outside the door and walked back to the car, feeling the breeze lift her hair. She felt joyful and free. She could be in control of it. She could leave this part of herself behind and be happy with Patrick.

Back home, still riding the wave of joy, Elizabeth took the prized notebook into her room and shut the door. Without looking at the pictures, she tore the pages out and threw them in a bin. She carried it down the stairs and dumped the contents into the trash compactor. Take that, fetish.

Chapter Four

Back in her dorm room, Elizabeth was idly playing on the internet instead of studying for the quiz coming up in her Algebra class. Cassie poked her head around the door. "Hey, study break time," she said. "We're going to the movies."

Elizabeth hadn't been spending much time with her dorm mates. According to her mother, college was the time when one formed the deepest friendships, yet it was her relationship with Amy that was deepening. It was hard to get close to these girls when she didn't feel she could talk to them about her dating struggles. This was a good opportunity to put in an effort at making new friends, though.

"Okay," she said, "I'm in." She grabbed her coat and a scarf.

The four girls caught a bus down to the movie theater. Cassie pulled out a magazine and they all huddled around it to read the gossip. "What are we seeing?" Elizabeth asked.

"Oh, whatever that new romantic comedy is."

Elizabeth nodded. It sounded good. Something where she wouldn't have to think. Her brain was too crammed with facts and figures from her classes. It was nice to get away and do something that didn't require her to put a huge effort into appearing normal.

The girls got their snacks and settled into the theater, sitting in one line with Elizabeth in the middle. Elizabeth's smile faded rapidly as a character in a wheelchair came on the screen. She sat up straighter; the movie now had her full attention. How could she not have known that this movie had a male paraplegic character in it?

At once she was torn. Ordinarily when she found something like this, she would make a mental note to get hold of a copy for her collection. Now there was no collection. She had destroyed it. And right in this moment the movie that should have been like porn for her made her miserable instead.

How dare this wheelchair try to sneak back into her life? Not only did she feel a burning jealousy and fear that she would never again have what the woman in this movie had such easy access to, but this was supposed to be a time away from the draining nature of her sexuality, a time to just relax with her girlfriends.

In the dark theater, people all around her, she felt tears gliding down her cheeks. The movie taunted her and no one else felt it. Elizabeth was deeply and profoundly alone. Why couldn't she be normal? For even five minutes? Was that too much to ask?

She thought of Patrick and how could she continue to date him when a wheelchair in a movie could do this to her? But he didn't have to know. She would put this experience out of her mind as quickly as she could. It didn't have to own her.

Her life never seemed to be in balance, it was always swinging between extremes. Either she felt totally asexual, no interest in it or she was like an animal in heat, obsessing and making herself sick. The heat was coming. There was nothing she could do to stop it.

Going home, Elizabeth was barely aware of anything around her. She couldn't follow the conversation of the other girls. There was a pounding in her ears and she just had to get home and be alone. She felt like she was falling into a bottomless, dark pit, desperately clinging to the edge with her fingernails, but it was hopeless. She had to just let go and allow the obsession to sweep over her. Would this happen for the rest of her life? Would there ever be relief?

The other girls walked slowly towards the campus coffee shop. Elizabeth mumbled an excuse and jogged towards her room. She collapsed on her bed and let her tears soak into the pillow. All the videos and pictures she had gotten rid of came into her mind. The photos were irreplaceable. "You dummy," she said to herself. "Did you really think you weren't ever going to need those things again?" She had been such a fool to think it was ever going to be gone.

She got up and went to her computer, staying up late into the night watching YouTube videos of wheelchair sports and feeling both the tingle of pleasure in her groin and also the tingle of self-recrimination in her stomach. The two sensations battled in the center of her body.

Whenever she thought the devoteeism was fading and it might disappear entirely it was always just hiding under the surface of her life. During those times when it was so in the background she thought she didn't need it, her sex drive also dived. It wasn't as though other sexual urges replaced those that were on a low ebb. She became basically asexual during those times the devoteeism wasn't strong. Even though she sometimes thought it would be nice to shake the desire for good, there was still a deep fear that if it were possible to get rid of devness, there would be nothing to take its place.

It was a moot point. As she fell back into desires so intense that she lay in her bed shaking, her face feeling like it was on fire, she knew it was never going to be gone. It was not a curable situation. At last she fell into blessed sleep and dreamed about Johnny Depp in a wheelchair.

Elizabeth almost didn't see Patrick as she came out of her Biology class. She was thinking about which assignments had to get done tonight and which could be put off, missing the unusually warm November weather and Patrick standing at the bottom of the wheelchair ramp with flowers in his hands.

"Oh," Elizabeth jumped as he moved toward her.

"These are for you," he said with a self-satisfied smile.

Elizabeth shifted her books to the crook of her hip and accepted the bouquet of carnations with one hand. "Thank you," she said. When Patrick's face fell she added, "They're very beautiful." She still saw disappointment in his face, so she continued. "It was very good of you to bring them."

"I looked up your birthday in the online directory."

"Oh. Thank you," she said again. She wondered if she better hurry and do the same, figure out when his birthday was. He walked her back to her dorm, and gave her a quick kiss on the lips. Elizabeth smiled at him as he turned to continue on to his class, but once his back was turned she couldn't resist the urge to wipe her lips off with the back of her hand. Her stomach felt slightly unsettled.

Elizabeth was much more pleased by the decorations she found on her door than by the flowers. The girls on her hall had put up a Happy Birthday banner just like Elizabeth had seen done for people in high school but had never been done for her. College really was a fresh start. Her new friends didn't realize that she was uncool. Or they didn't care.

Cassie peeked her head out from her own room and said, "Happy birthday!"

Elizabeth grinned. "Thanks," she said.

"Awesome flowers." Cassie came out into the hallway.

"Yeah," Elizabeth said. "Patrick gave them to me."

"So you guys are, like, serious?"

"I guess," Elizabeth said. Cassie took her books to hold while Elizabeth pulled out her key and opened the door. Cassie followed her into the room.

"He's perfect, Liz," Cassie gushed.

"Right," she said. "Perfect."

Elizabeth went home that weekend to celebrate her birthday. Her parents took it as an excuse to have a family get together. Bubby was there, but Grandma Margaret had a "prior engagement" as she put it. Cousin Libby was there with her husband and her parents. Amy and her family were invited too.

There was some fuss to get Amy's ninety-five year old grandmother's wheelchair into the house. Elizabeth stood back and watched. Even though it was just an ugly, old hospital-style wheelchair, and not sexy at all, it made her think about whether her parents would ever be willing to go through this trouble for someone Elizabeth cared about. But it was bad for her to think about that now. She was with Patrick. Patrick, who could walk right in the door, smile at her mother, talk books with her father. *Forget about wheelchairs*, she chided herself forcefully.

The party was not particularly fun for Elizabeth. It was a formal dinner in the dining room that was almost never used, then everyone sat around the living room and talked. Susan passed glasses of wine and handed one to Elizabeth even though it was only her nineteenth birthday. Libby refused her glass of wine, with a bashful look towards the floor. The room fell very still as she said, "Actually, I'm pregnant." She looked back up with a grin on her face and rounds of congratulations and toasts began.

Elizabeth sat quietly on the side next to Amy, her only friend at the party. She wasn't that interested in the wine and put her glass down on the floor beside her. She didn't congratulate Libby, not yet. She just watched and thought about what a perfect life her cousin had. It seemed charmed. Libby was pretty in a rosy-cheek-and-apple-pie kind of way. She found suitors easily and married a soft-spoken, cute young man, had a charming old townhome in Cambridge and now was starting a family. Elizabeth could imagine her sauntering down the lush, tree lined streets of her neighborhood with a tiny child in an old-fashioned pram.

As Amy's grandmother was pushed forward to coo over Libby, Elizabeth was snapped out of this fantasy by Amy pinching her arm and whispering, "Oh my God, you're not, like, attracted to Gran are you?"

"Ewww," Elizabeth said. "No! Why would you say that?"

"Well, she's in a wheelchair."

It took Elizabeth a few moments to form a coherent sentence, she was so startled. "Are you attracted to every single person of any age or gender who isn't in a wheelchair?"

"Oh. No, I guess not. I didn't think of it like that."

"Jeez, Amy! I'm not a slave to wheelchairs; they don't turn me into a zombie."

"Well, I'm only asking. I'm curious. How are things with Patrick?" Amy said with a big grin.

"Fine," Elizabeth said.

"That was enthusiastic."

"It's good, really, fine." Though she didn't say it, she couldn't help thinking: *he's no Stewart.* She shouldn't think like that. This was going to work; she was going to make it work. It made her mother so happy. Whether or not it made Elizabeth herself happy was just not relevant.

After seeing cousin Libby's life falling into place so beautifully, Elizabeth felt more determined to make sure that hers would too. When she got back to campus, she called Patrick on her dorm phone and invited him over. Instead of going out to the common room, she said,

"Come on in." He walked into her room, where there was hardly room for both of them to stand up. The bed was the most visible thing there. Elizabeth nodded her head at it.

"Really?" Patrick said. "Are you sure?"

"Yeah," she said. She climbed onto the narrow bed and stretched out, leaving space for him. Patrick lay down beside her and started kissing her. She did feel a little bit of tingling in her body when he kissed her. Nothing like what she had felt with Stewart, but a little bit. Hope surged in her.

She rubbed her hands over his arms and tried to imagine what was going to happen next. Could she let him into her body? She cringed a bit at the thought. Trying to imagine that his legs didn't work helped a little, until he shifted and climbed on top of her. He was heavy against her stomach. She looked up at him while they kissed and it felt odd. This was the first time a man had ever been on top of her. Stewart was the only person she'd ever slept with and she had always been on top. The edge of Patrick's jeans was rubbing against the skin over her hip bone.

His mouth was eagerly grasping at hers. She had an urge to press her head back into the pillow and pull away, but she suppressed it. "Hold on," Patrick said. He jumped up and began pulling his clothes off. Elizabeth pulled her own shirt over her head. Slowly she wiggled out of her jeans. Patrick was already naked and he walked back toward the bed with his penis huge, engorged, and dripping.

Elizabeth could no longer control the revulsion that was fighting its way through her body. She felt like she might throw up. She scrambled up and pressed herself back into the corner of the bed, desperate to get away from his body. There was no way she could let that thing inside of her.

Her body had no desire at all. Whatever moisture there had been was gone; Elizabeth was dry and closed off now.

"Patrick," she whispered, "stop."

"What do you mean? What's wrong?"

"I can't."

"Elizabeth?"

"I'm so sorry. I thought I could do this."

"Hey, it's okay," Patrick said. He sat on the bed and reached out to her, but all Elizabeth could see was his all-wrong body. Patrick continued, "Is it your first time?"

"It's not that."

"What then?"

He looked so confused and Elizabeth wanted to make it all fine, to find the words to explain. "I'm sorry. I just can't."

"But I thought. . ."

"You aren't my type. I thought I could do this, but I just can't."

It took him another several seconds before he began to put his clothes back on. Elizabeth didn't move. She lay in the corner of her bed with her knees pulled up to her chest and watched him leave. He looked at her with a hurt and confused frown, his shoes in his arms, and left her room. The door clicked behind him and Elizabeth let out her breath.

Hopeless, that's what she was. She lay on her bed and stared at the ceiling. This settled it; she knew for sure that her future was going to be difficult. Finding the man for her was going to be close to impossible. What a horrible realization to make at nineteen-years old.

Amy was right, though, now Elizabeth knew the truth. She would never be able to maintain a relationship with an able-bodied man. Devoteeism and she were stuck with each other for life.

Chapter Five

For Thanksgiving Elizabeth went home. As soon as she opened the door she saw her mother with a list in one hand and a broom in the other. All the relatives were coming, many more than had attended the birthday party, but Elizabeth was still surprised to find her mother cleaning. Susan had a service that came to do the cleaning usually. Elizabeth wasn't sure she had ever seen her mother scrubbing anything. Until today. Today Susan was frantic with things to do.

"Come in and try to keep off the carpet," she said. Elizabeth tip-toed towards her room. There was a chilly breeze airing the house out. Susan called after her, "When you've put your bag away, come and vacuum in the living room."

The rest of the afternoon was spent listening to Susan give instructions. "David, let the man with the food in. Elizabeth, clear off the sideboard in the dining room. Someone get the extra chairs from the basement."

In the midst of spreading the wine-red table cloth over the dining room table, Susan asked, "Did you invite your new boyfriend to come?"

Elizabeth looked away. She didn't have to say anything for her mother to know the truth, that there was no boyfriend anymore. "Ah well," Susan said, "chin up. There'll be another one."

Of course there would. Elizabeth didn't argue.

Thanksgiving was, like most get-togethers with her family, overwhelming and full of polite conversation that neatly avoided anything real. Elizabeth tuned out most of the conversation. She was distracted by the way the house seemed to have almost a double exposure.

Everywhere she looked she felt as though she could see two or even three or four different images at once. All the moments she had spent throughout all the years of her life were haunting the spaces of this house. Her months at college were wiped out and she felt child-like again. As though the ghosts of her previous selves were grasping her shoulders and trying to drag her forcibly into the past.

After everyone had finally gone home, Elizabeth found her mother relaxing in the living room. Relaxing for Susan involved draping herself elegantly in the stiffest chair and sipping a glass of wine. Was this how Elizabeth was expected to be? Was this the life that Susan was trying to lead her towards? She didn't want it, couldn't imagine herself in a house with stairs up to the front door, with a husband who walked. *Don't say anything,* Elizabeth instructed herself as she came into the room, *don't say anything, don't say anything, don't say anything.*

"Mom, I don't think I can ever be happy with an able-bodied man." Oops. She had an urge to slap her hand over her mouth, but tried to play it cool.

Susan gripped the edge of the chair and looked up at her. "That's insane; can you hear yourself? We can get this fixed."

"Stop talking like there's something wrong with me."

"There is something wrong with you! This is not normal."

"Fuck normal."

"Elizabeth!" As Elizabeth walked away, Susan called, "We are going to talk about pulling you out of school, or at least having you live at home!"

Elizabeth knew she couldn't just sneak back to school without talking about what she had said. She would have to calm her mother down so she wouldn't make good on the threats.

"I'm sorry about what I said," she told Susan the next morning. Perhaps now would be the time to tell her mother that this was a known thing, that there was a word for her attraction. Or maybe that would give Susan more ammunition for the thought that it was a condition, something that needed to be fixed and cured. Maybe Susan would use the word to look it up, to see the same scary things Elizabeth had seen, the terrible things people said about it online. She just had to let this blow over, not mention it again, stop discussing these things with her mom. Susan could never know that it had a word, that it was a full-blown, recognized fetish.

"Did you want to take the microwave back with you this time?" Susan said when Elizabeth came into the room.

Elizabeth sighed. "Yeah," she said. Having a real conversation with Susan just wasn't possible; she was too good at deflection. Why did Elizabeth even feel the need to connect with her mother? Couldn't she just leave it be? After all, who had a mother that actually understood? It wasn't even normal for your mother to know you fully.

In her room with the door closed she called Stewart on her cell phone. "Remind me that I'm a good person."

"Is someone suggesting otherwise?"

"My family."

He laughed. "Welcome to my world: where parents cause more problems than they solve. You've got to stop listening to them. You don't owe them anything."

"Yes I do! They're my parents."

"They're the ones who wanted to have children. You didn't ask to be born."

"What if they're right and this thing is bad?"

"I know it's scary, it was scary for me, but I'm convinced that it isn't bad. I have a more authentic relationship with you than I do with anyone else in my life; that wouldn't happen if you were simply fixated on my disability."

"Thanks," Elizabeth said with a sigh.

"You're okay," Stewart said.

"Yeah, yeah, yeah." She picked at the bedspread with her fingernails. "I tried to date an able-bodied guy, you know."

"How did that go?"

"Terrible."

He laughed again. "Be true to yourself, Elizabeth; you'll make yourself miserable otherwise."

Back at school, Elizabeth invited Amy over. She would have hung out with Cassie, but she had an idea and it was something that only Amy could help with. Amy was the only one who knew the truth about what Elizabeth wanted in a date.

Amy pushed open the door and cocked her head. "Okay," she said, "what's the big excitement?"

"Well, I thought that if I could find a good guy maybe my mom will come around. If she likes a disabled guy that I date, she might relax about it."

"I like the plan so far."

"I want to try internet dating. So I can specify exactly what I want."

Amy clapped her hands and grinned. "This is so exciting!" She rushed into the room. "I've been wanting to test out how internet dating works and now we can use you as a guinea pig."

"Great," Elizabeth said with mock sarcasm.

"You're going to need a picture, where's your camera?" Amy was already picking it up as she said this, Elizabeth's camera always being near her.

"Wait, wait," Elizabeth said. "We need to get a good lighting set-up." She tacked a white sheet to her wall and turned her lamps around to create a tiny photo booth. She took the manual camera from Amy and switched it with a digital and instructed her on what settings to use.

Once they had some good pictures, Amy sat at Elizabeth's computer and started searching for dating sites. "Oh," she said, "there are sites that are for disabled people specifically. Perfect!"

"Really?" Elizabeth looked over Amy's shoulder. Her friend was already building a profile for her.

"Look, you can list yourself as 'devotee' in the profile; it's one of the options."

"I'm not sure that I want to do that. It feels weird to attach this label to myself like that's all I am."

"Kind of like the label 'disabled'?"

"Good point. I guess it can't be bad to be upfront." Sometimes Amy's insight startled Elizabeth. Most people didn't put things together like that, but Amy was learning; she was making an effort to see things from Elizabeth's perspective.

"The other option is 'I'm not disabled, but I'm open-minded.'" Amy turned her head and gave Elizabeth an eyebrow-raised look. "If I saw that on someone's profile, I would assume they were a devotee who was too ashamed to be honest. Big turn-off."

"Okay, okay, put devotee in there."

"Next we have to describe you." Amy started typing and Elizabeth leaned closer to see what she was saying.

I'm a quirky artistic introvert. I'm a photographer and a student. I like quiet evenings and simple dates. I'm looking for a kind, independent, physically disabled man.

"That should be a good start," Amy said.

"Why did you put disabled in there? Isn't that obvious?"

"This site lists learning disability and bipolar disorder; I'm sure that's not what you're looking for."

"Oh, that's true."

It didn't stop them from writing to her, though. No matter how clear Elizabeth tried to make her profile that she was a devotee of *physical* disability, she got many messages from men whose disability was depression, autism, or learning disability. At first Elizabeth wrote back to each one to say that he was not what she was looking for, but as more and more flooded in and many of those she wrote to wrote back to try to convince her, she started screening the messages.

Each day when she came back from class she had emails from at least five guys. Despite the quantity, it was still difficult to find anyone even marginally attractive. Once 2NiceGuy40 found her he messaged her every day even though she didn't write back. The "40" in his user name was his age, making him more than twenty years older than Elizabeth. In his picture he was sitting on a big lazy boy chair, the top of his head was bald, he was significantly overweight and his skin looked greasy. His disability was listed as "stroke" and he did not appear to use a wheelchair. It mystified her that this man thought he had a chance with her. His messages were always a variation of "I'm a nice guy and stupid shallow women don't give me a chance, they're missing out." All Elizabeth could think when she looked at his picture was ewwwwww. Was this being judgmental? Was she supposed to give even disgusting creeps a chance? Other girls didn't go out with any and every man just so they wouldn't be accused of being superficial, right?

After ten messages from him she wrote back to tell him she wasn't interested since he seemed not to take her silence as a hint. Unfortunately writing back to tell him that he was too old for her did nothing but encourage him to keep writing. After another seven messages she told him she would report him for spam if he didn't stop. Eleven messages later she discovered that frequent messaging was not a qualification for spam on the site. Ten messages after that she told him that harassing a woman who wasn't interested by definition made him not the nice guy he kept insisting he was. Finally she just stopped opening his messages and deleted them when they came in.

Elizabeth was too nervous to go searching through the site, but so far the men who were finding her were not appealing, so she invited Amy over to give her courage. With Amy looking over her shoulder, Elizabeth searched through men in her age range with physical disabilities and was even more discouraged.

"This is depressing. The one decent-looking guy on this entire site is in California," she said, pushing her laptop away from her.

"It's not Stewart is it?"

Elizabeth laughed. "No. I'm sure he's not on the internet looking for dates."

Amy reached over her shoulder and clicked into her inbox. "Why do you have all these messages from fifty-year-old able-bodied guys?"

"I wish I knew," Elizabeth said. "My best guess is that they're here because they are beyond desperate and they assume that I am too. To be honest, I'm getting there. But jeez, if I wanted to take just anyone I would date Patrick or some other campus boy."

"Well, don't give up hope yet. It takes time to sort through all the crap, we'll get you there."

"Okay, enough of me and my pathetic dating life, let's go out and do something fun."

"Sounds good. Come on." Amy said, "Let's get out of here."

"Where are we going?"

"I'm going to do my hair, and then we'll walk over to the frat houses, I'm sure something will be happening."

Elizabeth knew immediately that she wasn't going to be finding any potential dates at the party they found.

There were ten stairs up to the entrance of the old brick fraternity house. Inside she sipped from a red plastic cup of beer and watched Amy shine. This was Amy's element. She flirted, she smiled and drew attention from the whole room. Amy didn't even have to do anything to draw everyone to her. Elizabeth had the opposite quality, an ability to fade into the background. It was useful at times like this when she didn't want any of these boys' attention.

Amy came stumbling back over, her hair disheveled and springing out around her head, laughing and grabbing for Elizabeth's arm. "Isn't this fun?" she said.

"Yes," Elizabeth said. It was fun to watch Amy.

Amy dragged her down the wall to the floor. They sat side by side, Amy happy drunk and Elizabeth hazily buzzed. "Do you think," Amy said, "that there are other people out there like you?"

"There have to be. There wouldn't be a word for it if I was the only one."

"It could be like one of those rare diseases that only show up once every couple hundred years."

Elizabeth laughed. When she could catch her breath again she said, "I doubt there would be as much worry and fear about it if it were that rare. I do feel really alone, though. I wish I knew even just one other person like me."

"Can you imagine?"

"What?"

"Huh? Oh, for other women like you that are older. They didn't have the internet and stuff and they might still think they're all alone. I bet there's a lot who can't even admit it to themselves. It was hard for you to and not everyone is as unflinchingly honest as you."

Elizabeth extracted the cup from Amy's hand. "You're making less and less sense; I think you've had enough."

"It's weird, though, it seems like what you are shouldn't happen, evolutionarily. Survival of the fittest and all that."

"Actually, evolution isn't that simple. I've been learning in my class that there are gay animals. Also, in every human society there are a percentage of women who never have children; it seems to be necessary for some reason we don't understand. So, evolution is far from a simple concept."

Amy rolled her head on the wall to look at Elizabeth and after a few seconds she seemed to have processed what she said. "Don't you want kids, though?"

"Maybe. But with today's technology that wouldn't be a problem. That wasn't really the point I was trying to make."

"There's always adoption, I guess."

"Exactly. I'm not going to worry about that. I'm only nineteen and I don't even know if I want kids yet! Besides, most disabled guys wouldn't have an issue fathering kids."

"This conversation is making my head hurt. Let's rate the boys instead."

"I think you have an advantage there."

"Just pretend that they're all in wheelchairs, okay? You rate them as though they're already paralyzed."

"Okay." Elizabeth smiled at how relaxed and accepting her friend was of this odd quirk.

Amy began ranking the boys at the party in order of attractiveness and Elizabeth gave her opinion on Amy's choices. She wondered if any of it mattered. Was there an attractive man in her own future?

Chapter Six

Elizabeth looked at her latest pictures. They were dull and lifeless. Where was the joy? Where was the energy? She was never going to be any good. At least next semester she would be able to take some photography classes. There had been no room for them her first semester, as she took core classes. Next term she would have two. Maybe there was talent buried somewhere inside her that teaching could bring out.

She took her camera outside and sat cross-legged on the ground, practicing focusing in on individual blades of grass. Snow had been late this year and so far, though it was December, they only had a flurry that had already melted. Still, it didn't take long before the cold seeped through her jeans and the hard ground made her butt sore.

Elizabeth felt like a talentless hack. Some days she wanted to give up on the idea of being an artist and look for a more practical degree. It would relieve her parents if she would declare a major in engineering.

Somehow photography always stayed with her. Ever since she had first discovered cameras, she had loved them. Her dad gave her a camera with a tall, detachable flash that burned out one cell at a time. Unlike what most children would probably do, she saved her pictures carefully. She saw the limit and waited for just the right thing to take a picture of. She hoarded each precious flash bulb.

She had never gone more than a week without taking a picture of something, though. She just couldn't stop. Regardless of whether or not she had talent, she would keep taking pictures because she couldn't not.

Her dorm phone was ringing when she got back inside. It was Susan. "Do you have your dress yet for Grandma's Christmas party?"

"No, not yet."

"Well, you better hurry up. Try not to pick randomly. The yellow last year wasn't flattering. You should get something green."

"Okay, Mom."

"I'll put some money in your bank account. Go this weekend or you'll run out of time."

"Okay."

Elizabeth walked to Copley Place and located the Neiman Marcus. As usual, she felt completely out of place. This was a classy store and Elizabeth was wearing her usual jeans and white t-shirt. She was always overwhelmed by these places and had no idea what to do. She stood in the front of the store under the bright lights, seeing them reflected in the white tile floor and wondered where to find a dress.

A sale's girl approached. "What can I help you with?"

"I need a dress. For a Christmas party. Something green."

"No problem. Let me gather some things for you to try on. Follow me to the dressing room."

Elizabeth breathed out a long breath and followed. She put on the first dress the girl brought and examined herself in the mirror. She was not used to analyzing her appearance. The dress was an emerald green in a silky material. It had no back to speak of and tiny straps. It pooled on the floor around Elizabeth's bare feet. She had to admit her collar bone looked nice.

"What do you think?" the sales girl asked.

Elizabeth came out of the room. "Is it weird that my hips are showing through?"

"You look beautiful," the girl gushed. "You could easily be a model. Most women would kill for your body."

"Um, thanks," Elizabeth said, feeling the heat rising to her face. "I guess I'll take it." Even though she wasn't sure what the point was, she would attempt to look beautiful for Grandma's party. She didn't even have a date; there was no one to look pretty for. But it would make her mother happy. And at least if she someday showed up with a disabled guy, her family wouldn't think it was because she wasn't pretty enough to attract an able-bodied one.

Back in her room, Elizabeth had an IM waiting for her from her dating site.

Hi there. I'm James. How are you?

Fine. How are you? Elizabeth typed back while she scooted her chair back with one leg and slid onto the seat.

I'm good. I work for a local cable TV station. I like to play with my dog on my days off. How about you?

That's really neat, Elizabeth typed. *You have a dog? What kind?*

She's a Labrador.

The conversation continued, light and easy and refreshingly normal. He didn't ask for a picture of her naked or ask for her favorite sex positions as some of the men IMing her had attempted. He didn't have a picture up, but his profile sounded kind and interesting, and best of all, he lived nearby.

Why don't you have a picture up? Elizabeth couldn't help asking.

I like to get to know someone by their soul, you know? None of that superficial crap.

Impressive answer. Elizabeth felt a little guilty for even wanting to know what he looked like.

Elizabeth messaged with him, enjoying a flirty banter after classes most days of the week. They

continued to talk when Elizabeth went home for
Christmas break.

The day of her Grandmother's party, Elizabeth
put on her new green dress and raided her mother's
bathroom cabinet for some makeup. She tested out some
of the techniques Amy had shown her. Instead of a
ponytail, she twisted her hair into a bun on the top of her
head.

"Ah," Susan said when Elizabeth came down the
stairs. "Much better." Then she noticed that Elizabeth
was holding onto her camera.

"You're not actually bringing that thing, are you?"

Elizabeth clutched her camera closer. "I always
do," she said.

"You're an adult now, Elizabeth. It ruins your
dress. Doesn't it, David?"

Her father glanced at her. "I'm sure it's fine," he
said. "It makes her happy; let her do it."

Elizabeth sat on the edge of one of the living
room chairs while her father searched for his keys. It was
the same scenario every year and they were always late.
Elizabeth suspected her mother was right when she said
that David misplaced his keys on purpose. Maybe not on
purpose, but he probably did subconsciously try to avoid
Susan's family, who were judgmental and very concerned
with appearances. Finally they were on their way.

After handing over their coats and entering the
ballroom, Grandma Margaret spotted them right away.
She seemed to float when she walked. As Margaret
greeted her parents, Elizabeth observed the stiff red dress
so dark it was almost brown and Grandma's extremely
white hair. It looked like fresh snow dusted with
powdered sugar and gleamed so much that Elizabeth
couldn't look directly at it. Her grandmother's skin looked
like delicate, thin pastry sheets.

"And how is school?" Margaret turned her attention to Elizabeth.

"Good. I'm studying photojournalism."

"Oh. Well, isn't that nice?" She looked at a loss of what else to say. Taking Susan's arm, she led her deeper into the party and left Elizabeth and David standing alone in the entrance. As they walked away Elizabeth heard Margaret say, "You must see Libby. She's just glowing."

Throughout the party people wanted to talk about nothing other than Libby and her pregnancy. Most would also quickly add that Elizabeth shouldn't worry, she would be next. With a knowing glow in their eyes, they would tell her that she would be in love soon. The look soon turned to a distant-eyed nostalgia as they remembered their own college days.

She wondered if they were right. Would James turn out to be the love of her life? She still hadn't seen a picture of him, but they had conversations that made Elizabeth feel more fully alive than in any of her other daily moments. It was his flattery that made Elizabeth's insides glow like the still-gleaming coals of a spent fire that is ready to flare back to life.

In between people coming over to gush about Libby, David asked Elizabeth about her pictures and her camera. It was a subject she felt much more comfortable with and David must have known that. Elizabeth was grateful for the chance to talk about something she actually had some experience in. The back of her mind continued to ponder what romantic future she might have and a tendril of hope was growing up through her body.

When she got back to campus she was ready to meet James in person. She felt a happy fluttering in her body. All possibilities were open in front of her. Amy came over to help her get ready.

"What do we know about this guy?"

"Not much, unfortunately. We've been chatting for a while, but not about anything too deep or serious."

"Hmm," Amy said, not sounding at all convinced. "What's his disability?"

"He said he has mobility problems and uses a wheelchair sometimes."

"And that's good enough for you?"

"I don't know. But I want to be open-minded and see if that will work."

Elizabeth put on tight jeans and a top with a cross of cloth across her chest. She even put on boots that had a little heel. She let down half her hair, since she usually wore it completely back in a smooth ponytail.

"What does he look like?"

"I don't know."

"How do you not know? Prejudging is one of the big advantages of internet dating!"

Elizabeth's ears got hot. She had been thinking how good she was for not being superficial, but Amy was not afraid to say that looks mattered. "He didn't have a picture," Elizabeth said, feeling defensive. "But we've been IMing and he seems nice. He's very flirty."

"I don't like this."

"Come on, you have to be enthusiastic with me, I'm nervous enough as it is."

"Okay. I'll trust that you know what you're doing. You look wonderful. Good luck."

Elizabeth walked to the coffee shop where they were meeting and stood outside in a dusting of snow, wearing a jacket much lighter than the season called for. She didn't want a bulky coat ruining her cute outfit. While she waited, she looked up and down the streets, hoping that his disability would be visible enough that she would know which guy he was.

Her hopes sank as a man walked toward her. There was no sign of any mobility trouble. In fact,

Elizabeth watched him walk from three blocks away without even the hint of a limp. If he was going to tell her he had mobility problems, shouldn't he at least fake it? She should just walk away now, but she felt like she had to give him a chance.

The closer he got the uglier he looked. He was at least fifteen years older than she and the hair was gone from the top of his head. His eyes bugged out slightly and he had wet-looking lips. He reminded her a bit of a toad.

How pathetic did you have to be to be hunting for dates on a disability dating site when you were not disabled? Of course that's exactly what Elizabeth was doing, but this guy wasn't a devotee, not if he was interested in her.

"Why are you so dressed up?" he said when he got close enough to her.

"I don't know." Elizabeth was startled and embarrassed by the question. "Because it's a first date?"

He grunted. "Should we go get coffee?"

"Um, sure," Elizabeth said. Really there was no date. There was no way she could ever date this man. He was disgusting. But she felt bad. She didn't know how to tell him that just from looking at him she knew she didn't want to go any further with him. So she reluctantly followed him into the Starbucks.

Once they had their drinks, they sat at one of the small tables. Elizabeth saw the looks of the people behind the counter. Everyone was wondering what a pretty young girl like her was doing on a date with this creep. They wondered what she saw in him, which was nothing. She felt trapped here.

Movement out the window caught her attention and she noticed a man in a power wheelchair in the distance.

"Did you notice that?" James said.

Elizabeth looked back at him. "What?" she said.

"That wheelchair. You always notice them, huh?"

There was no point denying it. She may as well try to make this man understand devoteeism the best that she could. "Yeah," she said, "I always notice them."

"Is it just a fantasy?"

"What do you mean?"

"Like do you think you really want an actual disabled guy? Or is it just some romantic notion about what disabled guys are like?"

"No, I want the real thing."

"How do you even know? Maybe you wouldn't like it in real life."

"I've been in a relationship with a paraplegic. It was great."

"Yeah? What happened?"

"That's really between him and me."

"You're really just a sadist, aren't you? You like other people in pain."

"God, no! I don't want anyone to be in pain. I think I'm pretty vanilla really." He didn't look convinced. She paused and thought for a moment. "Okay, maybe when I was younger I thought it was people's pain and suffering I was enjoying, but that was because society tells us that people who have disabilities have to be suffering. It felt impossible and far too shocking to think that maybe being disabled did not automatically cause suffering. I prefer people who are very adjusted to being disabled and are not suffering from it."

"Do you want to go back to my place? I've got a wheelchair there we could fool around with."

Elizabeth almost choked on her coffee. There was no way she was letting this man touch her. She didn't even want to know why he had a wheelchair lying around his place.

"Um, no."

"Afraid if you see me in a wheelchair you'll lose all control?"

Was he serious? Did he not know how hideous he looked? Did he think that a wheelchair was the only thing that mattered to her and if he sat in one he would magically become irresistible? Whatever, at least it was an excuse to get out of this horrible date.

"Yeah, sure," she said. She tossed her coffee cup in the trash and hurried out of the Starbucks before he could reach in for a hug. She walked quickly for several blocks, then slowed down her pace as she got closer to campus. Disappointment swirled around her stomach and she felt defeated.

He was yet another delusional man who thought he was way more attractive and appealing than he actually was. Where did men find this kind of confidence? Women were so quick to feel not pretty enough, not interesting enough, not something enough. All the men Elizabeth encountered online seemed completely sure of their own attractive power, even when they had none at all.

She didn't even look at her email when she got home. She changed into her pajamas and walked down the hall to the common room where a small group of girls was watching a movie and a few others sat on the couches with textbooks open on their laps. She wondered if any of them were having as much difficulty as she was finding a guy. Her inbox this week included a man who said that he had a brain injury and was looking for a lady who understood that he couldn't work, and someone whose message was only one question: what's your bra size? She couldn't help wondering if that technique ever got this guy anything. Did women actually respond to that? Why would he think that was an okay thing to ask? Did he expect to get a date from it? Elizabeth felt more confused every day that her profile was up.

"Why is dating so hard?" she asked the room in general as she dropped onto a couch and put her feet up on a chair.

"What are you having trouble with?"

"I can't find any good potential guys. I'm even doing online dating."

"Are you being too picky?"

"Maybe. I guess. What's the point of dating if you're not excited about it, though? I don't want to go out with someone I really already know I don't want."

"I met my boyfriend in my biology class," one girl said.

"I'm still with my high school boyfriend," another said. Several people said "Awww" at the same time.

It seemed no one else was having this trouble. She decided to try a popular dating site instead of the disability-specific ones. Finding a site that allowed her to search for keywords in people's profiles, she ran a search for "wheelchair" and came up with several men who talked about how in their free time they liked to help people in wheelchairs. Elizabeth raised an eyebrow. "Oh really?" she said to her empty room, "Trying to make yourself sound like an awesome person, are you?" In all of Massachusetts she found only one disabled guy. From his pictures she could see that he was a mid-to-high level quad, though not vent-dependent. That would be almost impossible to fake, so Elizabeth was pretty confident he really was disabled. Although, he could have stolen the pictures from someone else. She hated that she felt so suspicious now. But until she could figure out why James had wanted to impersonate being disabled, she wouldn't know if other people were doing the same.

Assuming that this guy was for real, it was not a disability Elizabeth had ever considered dealing with. It was one thing, she figured, to go out with paraplegics who could be completely independent, but a quad who was high enough level to need care was something else. This man had limited use of his arms and wouldn't be able to lift himself. He used a power wheelchair and she knew he must have aides to get him dressed and into the chair. Elizabeth was trying to be open-minded, though. Even if she was feeling skeptical, she would go on a date with him and see what it was like.

After the last guy that she spent so long chatting with and wasting time with, she wrote to this one suggesting to meet in person right away. They exchanged a few emails to get the basics down. He had been paralyzed for six years because of a motorcycle accident. He freelanced fixing computers for a living. She told him about being a devotee. It seemed far too dishonest not to. She didn't want him feeling self-conscious about his disability while she was actually enjoying it.

He had never heard of it, but didn't sound upset or put off by it either. He seemed to take the idea in stride. Elizabeth hoped that meant they could have a normal date instead of him just grilling her about her sexuality until she felt like an exhibit in a museum of freaks.

They arranged to meet at a different coffee shop. Elizabeth didn't like the idea of showing up at the same coffee shop over and over with different disabled men. Not that the first one had been at all, but she still felt less self-conscious if she went to a new place. And there were plenty of coffee shops to choose from.

She took less care preparing for this date than the last one. Since she was already unsure she really wanted to go out with a high-level quad, she wore her everyday outfit of jeans and a plain t-shirt with her hair in a ponytail. She walked to the shop with her head wrapped tightly in a scarf to try to hold back the bitter cold air and when she arrived she could see through the window that he was already there. No one was with him. He sat in a large power wheelchair that slightly tilted his body back. He was facing the door.

Elizabeth went in and smiled at him. "Theo?" she said.

"That's me," he said. "How are you?"

"I'm good, how are you?"

"Good." He lifted his left arm in what seemed instinctively to Elizabeth to be a gesture offering a hug and she leaned over him and put one arm around his shoulders before she realized that it was possible he didn't have that much motor control over his arms. When she stood back up he said, "So, you want to get something?"

"Sure," she said, relieved that he didn't make the hug seem awkward.

She stood back out of the way as he pushed against a joystick with the one hand that had a splint on it and turned the chair around. Elizabeth followed him to the line. At the counter they both ordered, he a coffee and she a milkshake, and he told her to pull his credit card out of the pouch on the side of his chair. Elizabeth followed his instructions and found the card. She carried both their drinks to the one table that didn't have attached seats and was stamped with a small access symbol. She moved the chair out of the way for Theo to steer his wheelchair into the space.

"Would you mind putting a couple sugars in my coffee?" he said.

"Sure," she said. She brought it to the counter and fixed it.

"Then you can wedge it between my legs," he said, "And put my straw in it."

Elizabeth was impressed by how relaxed he was telling her how to help. He made it easy to not feel like this was a big deal. As she gingerly put the coffee cup between his legs, she was suddenly aware of how sexy his legs were. She hadn't noticed them as much as she did with paras in their slick manual chairs. Theo was wearing jeans and his legs were thin and perfectly still. Elizabeth had a sudden urge to run her hands over them. She swallowed hard and got control of herself.

Once Theo had his drink situated, Elizabeth sat down beside him and sipped her milkshake.

"It must be tough, this devotee thing," he said.

Elizabeth smiled. "It can be. I make the best of it."

"Just like me," Theo said.

"Yeah." She was surprised he was able to see and acknowledge that being a dev wasn't simple or easy.

The time passed quickly as they talked about what movies they liked, what their families were like, and books they read. Theo had an e-reader and Elizabeth examined it.

"Easier for me to turn the pages on that," Theo said. She slid it into his backpack after she'd looked at it.

"Do you want to go to dinner?" he asked.

Elizabeth pulled out her phone and looked at the time. It was 5:30. "The date's going that well, huh?"

"I think so."

"Sounds great."

"Cool, there's a nice Italian place a couple blocks from here."

They had a nice dinner. Theo talked to the waiter in the same relaxed way to specify what he needed. Elizabeth attached a fork to his splint so he could eat. He was older than Stewart, but he didn't seem old enough to be creepy.

At the end of dinner, Elizabeth put her coat back on and prepared to go home.

"Do I get a kiss?" Theo said.

Elizabeth flushed. "Yes," she said. She braced her arms against the back of his chair and leaned over him, pressing her lips against his. His lips were soft and his breath tasted like coffee and cinnamon.

When she got back to her dorm she pulled out her phone and saw that there was a text message from Theo. *I had a good time tonight*, it read. *Me too*, she wrote back. She felt the glow of a new crush developing. Throughout the next several days she smiled at everything, even new homework assignments. She daydreamed about what a future with Theo would look like. Could she handle him needing help? Yes. She was now certain that she could. He was so at ease with it that it made her feel comfortable. And, it occurred to her, wasn't love and a good relationship worth the minor trouble of aides and caretakers? Even if someone with his disability wouldn't be able to help out as much, you could hire people to do almost anything, but you couldn't hire someone to love you. The whole thing felt very promising.

After a week went by she was a little surprised that she hadn't heard from him. She tried to shrug it off, to tell herself that he must be busy. Then she saw that he had been on the dating site looking at profiles. Okay, they had only been on one date, so there was nothing wrong with him checking out other profiles. A week later she tried calling him, but he didn't answer and he didn't return the call.

What didn't he like about her? Elizabeth thought they had a great date. She wasn't able to find out. She tried emailing him, but he didn't respond to that either. After three weeks it was clear that he was not going to offer an explanation, he was just going to disappear.

Elizabeth was miffed. Particularly since she had gone out of her way to be open to dating someone with a more severe disability than she was used to. She was willing to overlook some things in her quest to find a good relationship. Apparently he was not. Though what he would need to be overlooking, she didn't have a clue.

"Hey," Cassie said as Elizabeth came home from class one day. Elizabeth went into Cassie's room instead of her own and sat down on the bed.

"What's up?" Elizabeth said.

"I heard you talking about internet dating in the common room the other day. Just wondering why you're looking on the internet for dates? There's tons of boys right here. You're beautiful, you don't need the internet."

Elizabeth blushed. "Well, thanks, but there's a very particular kind of man I'm looking for and it's not easy to find."

"What do you mean?"

Elizabeth swallowed. This was her moment. No more avoiding. "Okay, I have this thing, this thing where I'm only attracted to men who are physically disabled."

Silence. Cassie just stared at her for several seconds. Finally she said, "I'm really not comfortable with that."

"Oh," Elizabeth said. She didn't know what else to say. She couldn't blame someone else for being disturbed by her and her desires. But it still stung. A lot. She could feel the self-hatred beating up against the wall she had built to shield herself from it. It was very close to getting in.

"Could you leave now?" Cassie said. She was looking at Elizabeth sideways, as though afraid of getting something contagious from her. Or maybe as though Elizabeth had just confessed to being a pedophile escaped from prison.

"Yeah," Elizabeth whispered. "No problem." She stood up and rushed out of Cassie's room. She already knew she would never be going back. Even though they lived across from each other, Cassie would ignore her,

pretend she wasn't there, and wait impatiently for the year
to end to get away from Elizabeth.

Chapter Seven

"This guy keeps asking when I'm coming to see him," Elizabeth told Amy over the phone. "He is really cute, but he lives in Georgia." Despite Cassie's reaction yesterday, Elizabeth was pressing ahead with her dating. Her own self-hatred, mirrored in Cassie's face, was threatening to break down her barriers, but she was fighting it.

"Don't do it, make him come to you," Amy said.

"Why?"

"These are guys and I know guys. Make them be the man and show that they are willing to go through some trouble to be with you. If you go to them, I swear you'll just be a nursemaid and a doormat to them. Make them man up. You want an independent type, right? Someone who doesn't give up and be lazy just because he's disabled."

"That's true."

"Trust me, I know men."

Elizabeth wrote back to the guy to say he should come see her in Boston. He never responded.

Every date and every possible date was more depressing than the last. Did normal people really believe there was only one person in the whole world for them? One soul mate? Did they have any idea how ridiculous it was? All they had to find was someone nice, someone with a good job, someone passably cute. They would never understand how impossible it was for Elizabeth. There was no fate, no guiding force that would find the needle in a haystack she needed to be happy. How would she ever find a man close to her age, nice, good job, things in common, lived in the same country even and had a spinal cord injury? Even if she did find this person, he would have to like her back. She would have to not scare him away in her excitement and desperation. The only ray of hope she could see was that maybe paraplegic men would be happy to be pursued, to be the object of that intense of a desire. Maybe they would be harder to scare off than able-bodied men. If she just knew where to find them.

Elizabeth decided that maybe she should back off on the dating. She had hoped to find someone her mother could like, but so far she hadn't even found someone that she could like. She would give it a rest and try to let nature take its own course. Besides, her school work could use more of her attention.

On the day she went to the disabled dating website to shut down her profile, there was a message from Jdog25 asking what devoteeism was. He asked in a very polite way, though, and Elizabeth resigned herself to being an ambassador for her difference; it was going to be up to her to educate men on what it was and she had the opportunity to try to spin it in such a way as to not sound scary. She wrote back to Jdog and said, "It's just an attraction. Like how some men like legs and others like boobs."

It was so much more complicated than that, but her explanation would be a start. A simple explanation without overloading him with information.

"All men like boobs," he wrote back, "and legs. There's nothing not beautiful on a woman."

Elizabeth smiled at that. They started writing emails back and forth. His name was Jared. She learned about his baby niece, and his techno-thriller reading habit. His picture was of him holding a beer in a sports bar. He looked knee-weakeningly cute. The only problem was that he lived in Virginia, at least an eight-hour drive away.

He asked for her number and she gave it. He took to calling her every night. By 7:00 each night she would make sure to be back from the dining hall and on the dot, Jared would call.

"I like your name," he said. "'Elizabeth.' That's beautiful."

"Thank you," she said, her smile changing the sound of the words. "I was named after my mom's aunt." She had always seen it as a nice gesture on her parents' part to name her after great Aunt Beth, who had no children of her own to honor her.

These days it was starting to feel more like a dire prediction, as though she were trapped by the name. Aunt Beth had never married and lived alone all her life, dying at age eighty-two. Elizabeth wished she had asked Aunt Beth more about her life when she had the chance. No one now knew why Beth had never married. There were some rumors about a man when she was a young woman, but then she had to take care of her mother. Someone had to do it. No one knew why it had to be Beth, one of five sisters and not the oldest or the youngest. It seemed to be believed in the family that Beth had sacrificed her own future in order to take care of her aging mother. No one could tell Elizabeth why.

The name was starting to seem like a curse, trapping her in that same life of unfulfilled hope. But maybe not. If Jared kept calling. "What do you do for fun?" he was saying now.

"I take pictures," she said. "I hope to make a career out of it, but it's also what I do for fun."

"That's cool. What do you like about it?"

"I love preserving life in images. It saves a moment forever."

"Artistic answer, I like it."

"Thanks. What about you? What do you do for fun?"

"Well, I used to ride four-wheelers. That's how I got hurt. Guess I'm still riding a four-wheeler in one way of looking at it. Now I go fishing a lot and I fix up old cars."

"Neat."

"Yeah. I should take you out on the water sometime, it's really peaceful."

"Sounds nice." It did. Elizabeth had never been an outdoorsy type, but she could learn.

The next day Elizabeth sat in class, holding a pen, but not making any notes. Even though it was a photography class, she was having trouble concentrating. She sat midway up in stadium seating. There were probably two hundred people in the class. On her way into the lecture hall the first time she had noted that there were cutaway seats for a couple of wheelchairs: all the way at the top next to the door, which was as far away from the lecture as you could possibly get. It didn't seem right to design a room like that.

Then Professor Higgins said something that caught Elizabeth's attention. "You will be working on one major project this term and the planning for it is wide open," she said. "This will be a major assignment, worth half--that's right, half-- your grade. It will go until the end of the semester. And, as if that isn't enough, one project will be selected to be displayed in an exhibit on campus at the end of the year. Gallery scouts will be invited to this event; the winner in past years has been displayed in galleries around Boston. Submit your proposals to me next week."

Even though class was over, Elizabeth didn't get up. She was already thinking about this major project. The lack of guidelines had her mind churning with ambitious ideas. She could do whatever she wanted. It was so exciting. An idea began to form in her mind and she jotted down notes for her proposal.

She emailed her proposal in several days early and got the go-ahead from Professor Higgins. This was going to be a great project. It would be perfect for her future portfolio and would start her in the direction of using the art of photography to further the disability rights cause.

After a couple of weeks of nightly phone calls, Jared finally suggested the idea of meeting. He said he was thinking about visiting a friend in New Hampshire and he wanted to stop for a couple days in Boston to see her.

"That sounds great. The only thing is you'd have to get a hotel room. My dorm isn't accessible."

"That's cool. No problem."

Elizabeth called Amy immediately. "You were right," she said. "I have a guy coming to see me. He's going to spend the whole weekend and he'll get a hotel room. We've been talking every day and I'm so excited."

"Yay! That sounds perfect," Amy said.

And when her mother called, she couldn't resist bragging about it. She was just too excited to not share the news with everyone.

"What are your plans this weekend?" Susan asked.

"Well," Elizabeth said slyly, "I have a guy coming to visit."

"I see. You're going to be safe, right? He's not staying with you."

"Yes, I'll be safe. It's not like there's any room here anyway."

"I don't like this meeting men from the internet. You have lots of nice boys right there."

Elizabeth couldn't repeat what she had already said at Thanksgiving, that she couldn't be happy with an able-bodied boy. It just didn't work. She had already told Susan this, but her mother had conveniently forgotten. Elizabeth didn't have it in her to keep bringing up the facts over and over until it sunk in. She would wait and if things worked out with Jared, then she could bring up the subject again with her mother.

Elizabeth arranged to meet him at a movie theater in the city. She put on the same outfit from her miserable date with James. It was a good outfit even if it had been put together for the wrong guy. As Jared rolled towards her, Elizabeth felt her breath catch in her throat. He was gorgeous, like a model in a black-and-white underwear ad; spiky brown hair, stubble on chin, sharp cheekbones, wide, dark eyes.

"Hi," he said, "I'm Jared. Wow, you are even more beautiful in person than in your picture."

"Thanks! Um, I thought maybe we could see a movie and have dinner and we should probably get you checked into your hotel, so maybe before dinner with that or after. And I can stay there with you. My room is seriously tiny and I've already tested it for wheelchairs." Elizabeth startled herself with this flurry of talk. She was feeling quite flustered. She wished she could explain this was not what she was usually like. But surely he would come to see that in time when they settled into things.

"I'm already checked in, so movie first is what I got out of that," he said.

Elizabeth laughed a weird, high-pitched laugh. "Right. Let's do it."

Jared bought them tickets. In the theater, he transferred out of his wheelchair and into one of the seats. Elizabeth sat next to him. Out of the corner of her eye she admired the wheelchair. It was the sleekest she had ever seen, like a beautiful piece of modern art.

After the movie they walked to a nearby restaurant. Inside, the hostess turned to Elizabeth and asked her how many and where would they like to sit. The woman's eyes didn't lower for a single second; she did not acknowledge Jared's presence at all. Elizabeth was still flustered, but managed to answer the questions.

At the end of a nice dinner, Elizabeth said, "Let's go back to your hotel room." It had been so many months since she'd slept with Stewart last and her body was crying out for release. She had to wash the memory of Patrick's naked body out of her mind, too. Though she had a paper due, she put it out of her mind.

Jared transferred onto the bed and turned the TV on. Elizabeth lay next to him on the bed, her head in the nook of his shoulder. It felt nice. While they watched a reality TV show, Jared's hand crept up under her shirt, played with one of her nipples.

"You're not wearing a bra," he whispered.

"That's right," Elizabeth said. She gave him her best naughty look. He pulled her face to his and kissed her lips. "You want to take my pants off?"

"Um, sure," she said. She crawled down to the end of the bed and fumbled with the button at the top of his jeans. She gently wiggled his unmoving feet through the legs and giggled while she pulled at the pants. Getting them past his hips was difficult, since he couldn't lift his butt to help. Eventually Elizabeth got them worked all the way off.

"Did you bring medicine or anything?" she said, remembering the injection that Stewart gave himself to get hard.

"No," he said. He touched his penis, trying to get it ready with his hand. Elizabeth was surprised that he would come to this situation so unprepared. He had been paralyzed for ten years; didn't he know how his body worked sexually? She sat back and waited, knowing that no matter how sexy she looked or acted, it wouldn't affect his body.

"Okay," he said, "I think it's ready."

Elizabeth threw one leg over him and lowered herself over his penis. She couldn't tell if it was even in her. She reached down with one hand to feel out the situation. Jared was losing hardness quickly. That combined with the massive amounts of liquid she was producing was making for no friction at all. She itched for relief.

"What's it doing?" he said.

"It doesn't seem to be quite working," Elizabeth said. "Let me try playing with it." She sat down beside him and worked her fingers over the soft flesh of his penis. Each time it began to get hard, it was soft again by the time Elizabeth got up onto him. He looked at her like he expected her to know what to do, like she was the expert on sex and spinal cord injury. She stopped trying to get the penis to cooperate and just rubbed herself against his body. She kissed the flesh of his neck and sucked on his earlobe, enjoying the sound of his little gasps of pleasure.

"Try it again," he said.

"It's okay," she said. "This feels wonderful."

"Let's just forget it."

"It doesn't bother me, really."

"Find something you like on the TV. I'm going to use the bathroom." He nudged her off him.

She took the remote, but watched as Jared pushed himself up with his arms and grabbed the seat of his wheelchair, pulling himself onto it without setting the brake. He backed out to the bathroom door and disappeared. Absently, Elizabeth rubbed between her legs. She was full of warm feelings. Even though it wasn't quite working, this was still the most satisfied she had felt in months. If only he would talk about it, they could figure out how to get things moving.

That night she slept pressed up against Jared, her right arm across his chest and her cheek on his shoulder. It was nice to be close to someone like that again and smell masculine skin, have strong arms hold her through the night.

In the morning, she opened her eyes and blinked rapidly in the sunlight coming through the gauzy white curtain. She was alone in the bed. Jared was across the room already packing his things up into a duffel bag. For a few moments she watched as he leaned over his still legs and reached with his huge arms to grab clothes from the floor.

"Do you want to get breakfast?" she said.

He stopped and glanced over at her. "Sure," he said.

They went down to the free breakfast in silence. As they rode the elevator, she expected for him to say something about the weekend, how he felt about it, how he felt about her. They had been talking every day for a month, so she felt close to him and yet also not. If only he would say something. She looked down at the top of his head, his perfect model hair, but he didn't say a word.

After breakfast he loaded his bag into his car and she leaned down to kiss him through the window.

"I'll talk to you later," he said and drove away.

She waited for some kind of follow up, but there was nothing. With a sickening sinking in her stomach, she realized her feelings were out on a limb all by themselves. He had never missed a phone call since they met, but today there was nothing. Elizabeth knew something was wrong, but she didn't know what or how to fix it without sounding clingy and desperate. What was it about her in person that he hated? Why couldn't he tell her? Why couldn't they talk about it?

Concentrating on her school work was tremendously difficult. Her mind refused to stop playing back the entire weekend, piece by piece, detail by detail, over and over. She thought of everything he had said indicating he was into her.

And none of it mattered. Something had negated it. Something had ruined it and she would never know what it was. Why were men so difficult? She couldn't do this anymore, really could not go through them disappearing.

She lay down on her bed and opened her phone, pressing the speaker button because she couldn't muster the energy to hold it to her ear. It sat in front of her on her bedspread and called Stewart. She wanted to ask him, "What's wrong with me that guys keep disappearing?" But he said, "I'm really sorry, this isn't a good time."

"What's wrong?"

"My dad had a stroke. I've been trying to help with him, but I'm exhausted."

"Oh, wow, I'm so sorry. Forget about me, I'm fine; go and help your dad. Let me know how it turns out."

"Thanks, Elizabeth."

She sat on her bed and leaned her head against the wall, gazing absently out the window. Disappointment pooled in her gut and she didn't know who she could talk to. She was sure Amy was tired of hearing about failure after failure. Her own mother thought there was something horribly wrong with her. None of her friends besides Amy knew what was really going on in her life.

Why couldn't she be normal? She got up and went to her computer, scrolled through Facebook to distract herself. She looked at pictures of her new friends at college. There were pictures of them with their boyfriends, laughing, playing outside, going to parties. It all looked so light-hearted and fun. Why couldn't she be one of them? Free to express her desires without fear. Why did it seem like everyone on Facebook was happier than she was?

Stewart called her back later that night. "Sorry about earlier," he said.

"Is your dad okay?"

"I don't know. He's such a stubborn ass. I think he'll be okay, but he won't listen to me, hates having me around. I don't know how to help him."

"I wish I could do something."

"It's just how he is. Nothing any of us can do. So, what's up with you?"

"I'm feeling really discouraged." Elizabeth sat on her chair and put her feet up on her desk, her long legs bent sharply, and picked at the skin on her knee. "These guys keep disappearing on me and I don't know what I'm doing wrong. It's wearing me out."

"It's not you. Believe me. Spinal-cord injured guys have issues."

"Yeah? Even though like three guys have disappointed me, you still think it's not me?"

"Definitely. You're in a difficult position. To you these guys are whole and appealing and just totally normal. For a lot of them, they're still dealing with feelings of unworthiness or frustration about their disability. Society has taught all of us that disability is worse than death. Recovering from that message can take years. Even a lifetime. Hang in there, Elizabeth. I've become convinced that your perspective is the right one."

"Thanks. I'm really grateful to have you to talk to."

"Any time. I do love you."

"I love you too. So how is your dating life going?"

"Oh, you know me. I'm not sure I'm the settling-down type. I don't know. There is someone, but who knows?"

"Aw. Maybe this is the one, the woman who can inspire you to be the guy who settles down."

"Have you been reading shitty romance novels?"

"I'm serious. I think love is out there for you."

"You too."

"I don't know. I don't think I can do it anymore. The outgoing, optimistic dater is too exhausting. I need to give up for a while."

"I can understand that. There are other things to devote your time to. Take a break and come back to it later. You're young; you have time."

"My life would be so much easier if I could date able-bodied guys."

"And you're sure you can't?"

"Oh yeah. Definitely. It might work short term, but I'm sure that eventually I wouldn't be able to resist cheating on him with a hot para. I know it's not supposed to, but sex matters to me. I like it; I want to be able to enjoy doing it with my partner. I can't settle for bad or no sex for the rest of my life."

"If you stop dating, no sex."

"At least there will be the possibility of hot sex in my future somewhere. I can't close that door. Besides, can you imagine how upset this mythical able-bodied husband would be to find his wife entirely uninterested in sex? How could I force someone I love to live that life? That's not love, it's selfishness."

"You have a point. And for the record, sex is supposed to matter to you. Who told you it shouldn't?"

"One guess."

"Your mother."

"You got it."

"You should stop listening to her."

"Right, because you're the relationship expert."

Stewart laughed. "One thing I'm certain about. Sex matters."

As Elizabeth hung up the phone she wondered if she had made a huge mistake giving up on Stewart. Was he the only chance she was going to have? As soon as she put her phone down it chimed with a text message. It was Amy asking what she was doing for spring break.

I don't know, Elizabeth wrote back, *I think I'm just going to go home and try to de-stress.*

Amy responded, *You should come with me. I'm taking a road trip to Florida to flirt with cute boys.*

I don't have the energy. Sorry, Elizabeth typed.

When Elizabeth arrived at home with her backpack, Susan said, "Why aren't you going somewhere with your friends?"

"I need quiet time to relax, not crazy parties." She hoped that her mother would allow her that quiet. Maybe she should have just stayed on campus all week by herself with some good photography books checked out of the library.

As far as she had tried to get from her childhood self, walking into her old bedroom again reminded her of how little progress she had made. She was more self-aware now, more solid in who she was. Yet that self-knowledge made her keenly aware of how unlikely love was in her future. She would probably stick close to home and become like Aunt Beth, a mysterious character that no one in her family quite understood.

Her mother, as predicted, did not leave her alone. Susan came into the room with something clearly on her mind. She always seemed to have a purpose behind every movement and every moment of her life. She also never knocked.

"Here's what concerns me," Susan said, and Elizabeth could tell her mother had been thinking some about Elizabeth's desires and their expression. "I don't like how you emphasize the physical aspects of looking for someone. What about inner beauty?"

It was actually a relief to be able to respond to her mother's concern, instead of trying to guess what those concerns might be and give un-prompted defenses. And Elizabeth had been thinking about these issues too.

"But outer beauty does matter. How can we try to pretend it doesn't? Luckily we all see beauty slightly differently. There are people I don't respond to and I can't help that. I'm not going to feel guilty about it. I'm not going to date a loser that I can't stand to make myself feel like a good noble person who only sees inner beauty. Here's the thing too, I've thought a lot about it, and there isn't this division that we seem to think there is that good-looking people are shallow and mean, and ugly people are nice with good inner character. It doesn't always work that way. I've met plenty of bitter, small-minded, mean, ugly people."

"You have some strange ideas about people, Elizabeth. I think you need to get a more realistic perspective."

"You mean I should look at disability the way that you do?"

"Don't get smart. You're young, you're idealistic, and you're naive. You have some crazy idea about handicapped people and it's not grounded in reality."

Never mind that she knew many more disabled people than Susan ever had. "Fine, that's fine. I am so done. I'm finished with dating." She thought, *No man will ever hurt me again.*

Susan opened her mouth to keep arguing, but Elizabeth guided her out the door with one hand on her mother's arm, and shut it behind her. This would make Susan happy. Giving up was the best option. It would get her mother to stop complaining. Elizabeth would just stop dating. Lots of people did it and lived their lives without a partner.

She could see her future. Alone. She would be the cool "aunt" to her cousins' children. She'd have an apartment, dedicate herself to work, enjoy late nights watching YouTube videos and touching herself.

She lowered her head and smacked her forehead against the closed door. It wasn't what she wanted. Not that anyone cared what she wanted. Maybe she could at least find someone to have sex with once in a while. Maybe Stewart would come to visit occasionally. It wasn't ideal, but it could keep her going in a life of disappointment. *No one cares what you want.*

No happiness. No husband and children and house. Alone. Alone. Alone. It wasn't fair. Why had she been hoping for fair? Millions and millions of people on the planet and wasn't it enough that many of them got the life Elizabeth wanted for herself? All she had done was get born, that didn't give her the right to expect happiness. Go through life, just get through it, one day after the next and it would be over. None of this would matter. The lump at the pit of her stomach wouldn't matter. She could just die and it would all be meaningless. With that perspective, why should she care what life brought her?

It seemed like such a simple want. What was so bad about wanting that simple life? She imagined what she could have had; what was the harm in it? She imagined Christmas with her family, sitting on the lap of a cute paraplegic. She imagined leaning back against him, whispering in his ear. She pictured a home, cooking in the kitchen when he came home and insisting on a kiss before she's let him taste the pasta sauce. She pictured sitting beside him while their children watched *Sesame Street*. Why was that so hard to get? How did life get set up this way? Why would anyone create a world where it was so difficult to get a happy life?

Could she be one of those women who lived alone and was satisfied with work? Could she make the world a better place and help other people to get their happiness? It was the only possibility right now. She could drive herself mad pursuing a dream that life didn't want to give her or she could start focusing her energy on helping other people live happy lives. Seeing people she cared about happy would be enough for her. It would have to be.

For the rest of the week, Susan did not mention boys or dating. Elizabeth tried to forget school work and spent time watching TV and studying other people's photographs on Google images.

She went back to school and spent weeks doing nothing but sleeping and working. She was in the lab or she was out taking pictures. Rather than living life, she just documented it and enjoyed finding the happiness of those around her. She spent late nights studying, and in the library she found photography books and studied composition. She forgot to wash her hair, just threw it into a ponytail and left it. How she looked didn't matter anymore. All focus on the work. All focus on creating a product that would live beyond her, that would mean something to others, others who could have the life she longed for. Others she could maybe show and guide. Her own life was insignificant now. Only the images mattered.

In her dreams, though, she still had trouble tuning out her disappointment. She couldn't get to sleep she was so tortured by her desire. She started taking NyQuil to knock herself out.

There was a hole in her that she thought would be healed by knowing herself and accepting what was in her heart. It wasn't that simple, though. The hole may have shrunk somewhat, but it wasn't gone and its edges were ragged.

Chapter Eight

With the help of Disability Student Services, Elizabeth put up fliers and announcements for models on her photography project. With her new plan to throw herself into work and forget about having a happily-ever-after with a guy, this project could not have come at a better time.

While waiting for the next step, she spent all her nights in the library studying photography books. She sat on the floor with huge books spread open in her lap, looking at perspective and lighting and composition. It reminded her of when she was a young girl, maybe ten years old, hiding in the basement of her hometown library with the autobiographies of various disabled athletes that she was too nervous to check out and take home with her. Back then she had known there was no hope to have a man like that in real life. She had been spoiled by her unlikely meeting with Stewart and the relationship that followed. How could she go back to fantasy after that? She leaned her head back on the stacks and closed her eyes. She let the moment wash over her, then looked back at the book in her lap. This was here and now and she had work to do. Work that was more important than Elizabeth and her personal desires.

On the day specified by her fliers, Elizabeth stood outside the tall oak doors leading into the conference room at the student center. On the other side were, hopefully, the people who could help her create her greatest project yet and satisfy her ambition to get the coveted art exhibit spot. She gripped the camera that was hanging from her neck and took a deep breath. She was ready. She reached out and swung open the door.

Quite a few people had responded to her call for models and Elizabeth was relieved. Part of her had suspected she would open the door to find an empty room. She wove her way to the front, past more wheelchairs than she had ever seen in one place before. Like spark plugs, little shots of excitement pulsed through her, but she ignored them. This wasn't about sex, this was about social justice and Elizabeth was going to do her part. More than her part, if she could.

"Hello, everyone," she said. "Thank you for coming. Here's what I'm looking to do. I want each of you to think about some silly little talent that you have, like touching your tongue to your nose or juggling. Anything fun and light-hearted. I'm going to sign you up for times to come in and model. I will also be doing casting for non-disabled models and older models. I will take all the pictures and blend them into a portfolio designed to show the common human spirit. If this sounds like something you would enjoy being part of, please come up to the table and sign up for a time."

Elizabeth sat down at the table and a line formed. She signed people up and was friendly and professional, but she did notice the cute boys in the room. One in particular stood out. He hadn't come into the line yet, but was sitting and watching. He was thin and gangly with a flop of curly brown hair over his forehead and deep brown eyes. His face was clean and boyish. She was so mesmerized by him that she almost forgot to sign up the person in front of her.

After most people had left and the line dwindled down to nothing, the cute boy pulled forearm crutches from under his seat, stood up and came towards her. He used the crutches very differently from how Stewart did. The one time Elizabeth had seen Stewart use crutches like this, he dragged his body with them, almost substituting his legs with them because he was completely paralyzed. This man moved more quickly, using the crutches for balance, it appeared. He almost seemed to throw himself forward and his body moved dramatically both vertically and horizontally with each step. The crutches hit the ground one at a time with a dull thump against a low carpet.

Elizabeth glanced down at his feet. His toes didn't lift all the way off the ground, but rather his feet dragged the ground and each time he took a step, the foot in back bumped against the foot in front in a fight to get ahead of it. His knees had a slight bend in them at all times and his legs seemed to be shaking slightly. Yet, he moved quickly.

He leaned on the table and took one of the pens, writing down his name. His fingers were tight and he gripped the pen in a way Elizabeth had never seen before. He lifted his eyes from the paper and met hers. He smiled. She sat on her hands and smiled back. When he left, Elizabeth peered over at the sheet. Ethan. She was going to enjoy his photo shoot.

She watched him as he walked out of the room, then she gave herself a little shake and gathered her papers. There was a happy, warm glow in her as she clutched the sign-up sheet. This was going to be a fun and unique project. She was sure no one else in her class would have something to match it. Even Cassie's giving her a dirty look on her way out of the dorm as Elizabeth got back couldn't dull her spirit.

In her room, Elizabeth marked each person into her calendar. She was going to be booked solid with photo shoots for the next three weeks. When she got to Ethan's name she smiled, remembering his sweet face and milk-chocolate eyes. She pinched the flesh beside her thumb. She could not flirt with him. This was always her downfall, giving too much of herself to boys because they were cute. Her resolve would hold. He was just another guy waiting to let her down.

On the day of his photo shoot, Elizabeth was already in the studio, having finished three appointments

so far that day. "Welcome. I'm Elizabeth," she said,
holding out her hand like a professional. Ethan let go of
the handle of one crutch and shook her hand. "I'm
Ethan," he said. His words seemed to hang for a second
as each one started. It wasn't quite a stutter, but very
close.

"Come on in."

The studio was small, but well set up. There was a
white canvas wall that spread down onto the floor and
several tall lights around the outsides. A stool and a couch
were in one corner. A table had a computer and a large
monitor to display pictures on the spot.

Elizabeth could almost imagine that this was all
hers rather than a space she reserved from the school and
had to share with all the other photography students. This
is what she hoped her adult life would look like: her in
her jeans and white t-shirt with two cameras around her
neck in a bright, uncluttered studio.

She backed up and Ethan came into the room.
She indicated for him to go to the white wall. There was
another student helping her with lighting. Elizabeth
consulted her sheet of paper. "Okay, so your funny talent
is tongue shapes, right?"

"Yes," he said.

"Great. Let's start with some regular shots."

He leaned forward on the two crutches, his
shoulders angled in and his hair fell in loose brown curls
across his forehead. It was the sexiest pose Elizabeth
could imagine. She licked her lips and kept the camera in
front of her face.

After a few snaps of Ethan standing and looking
at her he said, "What do you hope to do with
photography?"

Elizabeth paused, resting the camera against one
bony hip. None of the other models had asked her
anything about herself or about the project. "I want to be

able to say I was part of something great," she answered eventually.

"Don't we all?" He smiled. Elizabeth felt her insides melting and a pleasant ache radiated around her stomach. His smile was so easy and wide.

"Okay," Elizabeth said, looking at him through the view on her camera, "stick out your tongue!"

Ethan laughed, and looked down for a moment, then he raised his eyes to her and twirled his tongue into a clover shape.

Elizabeth snapped a round of pictures, moved to another side of him and did it again. "Hold it," she said. "I'm switching cameras." She put down the film camera and picked up the digital. When she had all the pictures she wanted, she thanked him and plugged the camera into the computer. Rather than leave, Ethan walked over and stood beside her, peering over her shoulder at the images.

Elizabeth leaned over the keyboard and zoomed one in. "What do you think?"

"Hey, I look pretty good. You're a genius."

Elizabeth laughed. "You can take some of the credit for that," she said. With him so close to her she could smell a musky pine-tree scent on his skin. While she felt his presence vibrating next to her, she kept her eyes on the screen, looking at his fixed image. He had a boyish, geeky face that Elizabeth found adorable.

"What was the other camera?"

Elizabeth turned to him and straightened up. "My film one. I want to develop those and get a good grain on them. I'm thinking of testing out a '70s feel."

"Cool. I'm thinking about majoring in photography too."

"Really? I haven't seen you in my classes."

"I did this one last year."

"Oh, yeah? What was your semester project?"

"It was dumb. I couldn't come up with a good idea."

"It is really hard to find a topic," Elizabeth agreed. "I spent years photographing odd things or normal things in odd ways, trying to find something that had meaning."

"Exactly."

Before her inner censor could stop her, Elizabeth said, "Say, would you like to help me develop the film pictures?"

"Yeah, that would be cool."

Later that week Ethan and Elizabeth worked side by side in the red-tinged darkness. They worked well as a team immediately. Each time Elizabeth needed something, it seemed Ethan was already prepared with whatever it was. She passed him dripping wet papers and he hung them on the drying line. He let her hand brush against his as she handed them to him and she felt an energy sizzling between them. Her lower body felt like it was slowly melting, a candle dripping from the flame of attraction. She could hardly mix the chemicals correctly because she didn't want to take her eyes off him. All she could think about was wrapping her arms around his waist, pushing him against a wall and pressing her lips on his.

When the last picture was finally done Elizabeth put her hands on her back and stretched. She and Ethan were sitting side by side on wooden stools and looking over at their handiwork, pictures hung around their heads like clothes on a line. They had worked late into the night.

"Maybe we should go get something to eat," Ethan said.

There would be no better opportunity than this. If she wanted to transition whatever was starting between them from friendship into something more she had to decide right now. They had so much chemistry it would be crazy to refuse to date him just because other men had hurt her. If she really did shut herself down from dating completely then she might miss the perfect opportunity, the right man for her.

More than anything, in this moment she wanted to go out with Ethan. But she couldn't do that without being honest. She couldn't imagine dating someone who didn't know that what most other girls would be uncomfortable with was the thing that made her want him the most. It wasn't fair to keep that from him. He had to know the truth before he decided if he wanted to go on a date. She had learned that from her experience with Stewart. She had tried to conceal her sexuality from him and when he found out it had really frightened him.

Ethan was still looking at her. "Listen, Ethan, I need to tell you something." Elizabeth licked her lips.

Ethan sighed and smiled a small, resigned smile. "Right," he said, and he reached down to pick up his crutches, hoisting himself up. "Don't bother. I know you don't feel that way about me; I'm just the crippled guy you hang out with to make yourself feel like a good person. Got it."

"Ethan, wait." She darted in front of him, blocking the door. He leaned forward on the crutches and fixed her with a stare. She said, "It's actually kind of the opposite."

"What do you mean?"

"Do you know what a devotee is?"

"Like a devotee of Krishna?"

"Um, no. A disability devotee."

"Huh?"

"Okay, here's the thing." She ran a hand through her hair, mussing the tight ponytail, and hoped she wouldn't burst into tears, the intensity of her desire and her fear of rejection tearing out of her. "I'm attracted to men with disabilities."

"You're what?" His eyes widened.

"Please don't hate me. I don't want you to hate me."

"Why would I hate you? So far this is sounding pretty awesome."

"Really?" Elizabeth said.

"Yeah, absolutely."

"I think you're really hot," she said.

Ethan grinned.

"I didn't want to hide it from you, I wanted to be honest."

"Hey, that's been the only thing challenging my dating life. With most girls, you're afraid of something coming up that she can't deal with. You try to minimize the impact of the disability, but it does come up. And you wonder if it's too much of a burden. So, let's go on a date."

"Okay. Let's do it."

Hope was opening one eye slowly within her. It was hard to have enthusiasm for Ethan, knowing how many times she had been disappointed. How many men had been excited at the thought of a dev and then disappeared with no explanation.

Chapter Nine

"What's open at this time?" Elizabeth said, grabbing her jacket from the corner of the dark room.

"There's a Denny's just a few blocks east."

They walked side by side and Elizabeth breathed deeply of his pine-tree scent. She watched him walk from the corner of her eye and it gave her shivers all up and down her body.

"So tell me more about yourself," Elizabeth said.

"Um, I don't know. I'm a sophomore. I haven't decided on a major yet. I'm an only child. Oh yeah, and I have cerebral palsy."

"I'm an only child too. My parents wanted another, but they miscarried."

"My mom raised me alone."

Though it was night, as soon as they left campus there was a glow all around of late-night businesses, neon closed signs, and street lights. A bus drove by, the two people on it clearly visible through the bright windows.

"I can't imagine my mom without my dad," Elizabeth said. "They balance each other out somehow. Did you know your dad?"

"No. He left when I was a baby. It's always been just me and Mom. I think she's having empty-nest pangs with me being at college. She can be kind of protective. Par for the course when you have a disabled kid, I guess."

Ethan held open the door of the Denny's for Elizabeth and they went inside. Once in the building it could easily have been the middle of the day. There was nothing to give away the late hour. Elizabeth ordered pancakes and hash browns while Ethan got a burger.

He picked up a stray flier left on the table advertising a new movie. "What is it with all the movies these days capitalizing on our nostalgia? They're turning every cartoon I ever loved into a movie."

"I know! I feel a little played," Elizabeth said. "But I'm also hopeful that maybe this means they'll come out with a live action *Extreme Ghostbusters*."

"I watched that; it was a good show. Not many people saw it, it seems like."

"It had a hot paraplegic guy in it."

Ethan burst out laughing. "Hot for a cartoon, eh?"

"Exactly! Hot for a cartoon."

"I had forgotten that character. I guess that was your favorite one."

"Definitely. Garrett was going to win the love triangle; I don't care what all the fanfic putting Kylie and Eduardo together says."

"You'll have to write your own fanfic."

"Nah. I'm bad with writing. My papers for English class are always too short. I like pictures a lot more. I can say more with pictures than I can with words."

"I have a great idea. We should make our own *Extreme Ghostbusters* cartoon. Instead of fanfic, do fan video."

"That sounds like a lot of fun."

He twirled a French fry in ketchup, holding it awkwardly between his middle finger and thumb, and said, "So you've been out with disabled guys before?"

Elizabeth nodded. "I've had several disastrous dates over the last year. Before that I had a para boyfriend. Stewart. We're still friends."

The fry dropped back onto his plate and Ethan stared at her. "Wait a minute. Your ex-boyfriend is Stewart Masterson, the surfing legend?"

"How did you know that?"

"I heard his speech last summer. And *New Mobility* magazine had a cover story on him just a couple months ago." Ethan became quiet, his brow furrowed, and he clinked his fork against his plate absently.

"What's wrong?"

"Nothing. I just can't believe you dated someone like him. I'm not athletic like that."

She reached across the table and took his hands in hers, her skin tingling at the contact with his flesh. "Ethan, Stewart and I broke up because we didn't have anything in common."

"You still talk to him?"

"Sure I do. He was my first boyfriend, first love, first everything."

"I don't like him."

"Oh come on. Are you kidding me? You read a magazine article about him, you don't know him."

"I just didn't know you went for athletic types."

"I don't. That's why I'm not with him anymore."

"So do you like wheelchairs better than crutches?"

Elizabeth paused from eating to consider this. "Wheelchairs were my first attachment, I'd say, and I love the way they move, their grace and shape. But I think how you walk is really sexy."

"I have a wheelchair I use sometimes. A lot of times it's easier, but people see wheelchairs as a sign you've given up. My family gets upset if I'm not doing everything I can to be upright."

Elizabeth giggled. "I don't get it," she said.

"It's nice to have both. The wheelchair lets me handle distance better and I don't fall over, but I can do stairs with my crutches."

The waitress walked back over. "Would you like dessert?"

Ethan and Elizabeth looked at each other. "What do you think?" Ethan said. Elizabeth pointed to the Oreo sundae. To the waitress Ethan said, "We'll share one of those."

Elizabeth smiled to herself. Sharing dessert, was there anything more romantic than that?

After the meal they walked back towards Elizabeth's dorm very slowly. It was early morning by now, still well before sunrise and the few other people out on the campus were stumbling by in drunk clusters. Crickets hummed in the air. The sidewalk was lit by white lamps every several feet. Elizabeth was very quiet, enjoying the sound of his crutches thumping on the pavement and the fronts of his shoes scraping the ground with each step. Finally, though, they arrived at the entrance to her building. She stopped in the doorway and turned to face him.

"I had a really good time," Ethan said.

"Me too," Elizabeth said.

He pushed his crutches inward and surged forward to her mouth. She could taste the cold rush of vanilla ice cream in his breath. His hair tickled her forehead and smelled of coconut shampoo. Everything about him was yummy. She engaged in the kiss, parting his lips with her tongue, and she touched his shoulders, running her fingers across the back of his neck. Her whole body was tingling.

She released his lips and rocked back on her heels. "Good night," she whispered. She walked into the building, hoping that he was watching her and resisting the urge to turn around.

Elizabeth changed into sweatpants and an over-sized t-shirt and lay on her bed looking at the ceiling. The universe was so strange. As soon as she had declared she was giving up the hunt for a boyfriend, a perfect potential showed up. Not only was Ethan cute, but he was close to her age and they were interested in the same things. It was very promising. Elizabeth slept well that night.

The next day Elizabeth was at the photo studio again and Ethan stopped by, inviting her to come over to his room to watch a movie that night. She promised to be there when she finished work on her project for the day. After he left, she found herself too distracted to get much more work done, though.

Earlier than planned she headed towards Ethan's dorm. She stopped by at the campus convenience store and picked up some chips, cheese, and crackers. When she got to his room he was already flipping through channels on the television. Elizabeth spread out the food on his bedspread and sat down on the other end of the bed with her back against the wall. He showed her his DVDs and she picked *Airplane*. After he put it in, he came back and leaned his crutches against the bed-frame, then sat down close to her. Close enough that their bodies were touching. She lay her head on his shoulder and he put an arm around her. She hadn't felt so comfortable with someone since months into her relationship with Stewart. They passed the food back and forth and laughed over all the same jokes in the movie, saying most of the lines with the actors.

After the movie ended, Ethan said, "You know, the last girl I dated told me she was fine with my disability, that she didn't even notice it and it made no difference to her."

"Oh yeah?" Elizabeth said. She shifted around so she was sitting cross-legged on the bed and looking at him.

His eyes were cast down at his lap and his twisting fingers. "Yeah. And she'd be fine when we were sitting down at a movie or a restaurant, but then I'd get up and she would look pretty mortified by the way I walk."

"Really?" Elizabeth tried to put herself into that mindset; she really tried to understand not liking the way Ethan walked. She couldn't do it. His movement was gorgeous and made her want to pounce on him and tear all his clothes off.

"I guess she couldn't be honest with me or with herself either. She probably liked to think of herself as the kind of person who doesn't see disability. She would say she could see past my body. What kind of shit is that? Why would I want someone who can look past what I look like? I want to be with someone who likes my body and whose body I like."

"Sounds reasonable to me," Elizabeth said.

"Until you I had no idea it would even be possible for someone to like my body."

"I'm really sorry you had to feel that way. It sucks. I wouldn't want someone just putting up with my looks either." She reached over and touched the side of his face, brushed his hair back from his forehead, though it fell right back.

The sun had set and the only light in the room was the DVD menu glowing on the television.

"She hated the way my legs shake," Ethan continued. "She tried to pretend she didn't care, but I could tell."

"Well," Elizabeth said, "she's gone now."

Ethan met her gaze. "You're right," he said. "Sorry. No more ex talk. I definitely don't want to hear about yours."

"That's so unfair."

He laughed. "If you have something bad to say about Stewart Masterson, I'm all ears."

"No, sorry," she said. "I got nothing."

Ethan pulled his body closer to her again and put his hand on her leg. Elizabeth recognized the eager look on his face and leaned in for a kiss. His warm breath tickled her lips. She clutched his back, felt his muscles through his shirt. He caught his fingers in her hair trying to pull her ponytail out. She pulled back as he fumbled with the bottom edge of her shirt.

"Can we not go right to the naked stuff?" she asked. The dim light behind him was casting shadows across his face.

"Oh," he said.

"I don't want to hurt your feelings," she rushed to say. "And I do think you're really attractive, I do. I just need to go slow. I've had a lot of disappointment."

"Sure, I understand."

"It's okay?"

"Yeah, whatever."

"This is nice," she said, trying to recover the mood.

He grunted and turned back to the TV, ejecting the DVD and switching it to Comedy Central.

"Um, I think I'm going to go," Elizabeth said. "Call me tomorrow?"

"Sure," he said.

On the walk back to her room, Elizabeth pulled out her cell phone and called Amy.

"What have you done with my friend?" Amy demanded.

"Hey, Amy."

"Is that you, Liz?"

"I know, I know, I haven't called enough."

"I hope there's a good reason. And by good reason I mean a guy."

"Yeah, there's a guy all right." Elizabeth held the phone away from her ear as Amy squealed. "I'm not totally sure about it," Elizabeth warned her.

"When are we ever totally sure? That's part of the excitement of passion."

"Right, well I'm starting to worry that he might only be interested in me because he thinks he won't have to work as hard to get sex. What if he just likes the idea of some freaky kinky sex fetish and not me?" Brittle leaves revealed after the snow thaw crunched under her feet and she kept looking around as she walked to make sure no one was close enough to hear what she was talking about.

"I don't know. It's a valid concern, but I haven't met the guy."

"You're not helping."

"Okay, well, look at it this way, you and he are both in the same position. You worry that maybe he's not seeing you but just some fetishist and he's worried that maybe you're not seeing him but just his . . . what's his disability?"

"Cerebral palsy."

"Okay, yeah, that. So you both have the same reason to be concerned and you're just going to have to trust each other. Besides, what's the worst that can happen?"

"I go off the deep end and sink into total and utter hatred of all men for all time?"

"Yeah. Don't do that. Don't let the bad guys win. You've got to keep your heart open."

"Aw, you're such a romantic, Amy." Elizabeth held the phone against her cheek while she pulled out her keys and got into her room.

"Just jump in," Amy said, "That's life. Don't risk the future because of things in your past."

Amy was right. Elizabeth hung up the phone and hoped Ethan wasn't feeling stung by her brushing him off. That wasn't what she had intended to do; she was just nervous.

All the next day she waited for him to call, afraid to make the next move since she had asked him to call her. She wondered what he was thinking, if he was upset, if he was giving up on her. Did she screw it up already? Just by being cautious? Was trying to protect herself the worst choice she could have made? She knew now that she wanted to go for it with him. If he ever called, she would be ready to show him just how sexy she thought he was.

Finally, in the afternoon Elizabeth broke down and called him. She took it as a good sign when he answered. "I'm sorry about last night," she said. "Will you come over this evening?"

"Sure," he said. "Don't be sorry. You can take whatever time you want to. I didn't mean to pressure you."

"It's okay."

"All right, I'll be there in a bit."

Elizabeth scrambled to get ready. She wanted him to really know how serious she was, how much she liked him. She pulled on a long t-shirt and left her legs bare, the shirt just barely grazing the tops of her thighs.

When there was a knock, she opened the door just a crack, and more fully when she saw that it was him.

"Oh my God," Ethan said.

"Hurry and come in," Elizabeth said, holding the door open for him. "I'm sorry about yesterday."

"Yeah, I can see that."

"Too much?" She bit her lip and felt a blush rise onto her face.

He walked closer and said, "Absolutely not."

She wasn't sure who initiated the kiss, but within moments they were eagerly grasping each others' lips. Elizabeth felt her lower body melting and she wanted nothing more than to have him inside her as quickly as possible. She pulled at his shirt, but he couldn't lift his arms without letting go of his crutches and losing balance. "Come on," she said, letting go of him and moving to the bed, pulling her own t-shirt off and throwing it onto her desk. She had nothing on underneath it.

"Oh my God," Ethan said again. He walked to the bed, put his crutches aside and sat while he pulled his shirt off. Elizabeth crawled to him and kissed the bare, salty skin where his neck met his shoulder.

"Do you have a condom?" she whispered.

"No."

"Oh, for goodness' sake! You have to go get one."

"Me?"

"Yes, you. They have them free at the student health center." Elizabeth folded her arms and waited for him to wiggle back into his shirt. She watched while he heaved his body up with his crutches and dragged his feet towards the door.

She lay back on the bed, laughing. She had never felt so relaxed and comfortable while naked.

He came back a few minutes later and they resumed where they had left off. As his fingers struggled with the condom, Elizabeth took it and put it on him.

"You can feel everything?" Elizabeth asked.

"Yes." He ran his fingers through her hair.

"That's different for me."

"Is it a problem?"

"No, I was just curious." She trailed her hands over his chest, stomach, legs. An urge came over her to grab hold. She couldn't get him inside her fast enough. They fumbled with clothes, pulled them off inefficiently in their desperation. Ethan wiggled his pants further down and revealed plastic braces on his lower legs. Elizabeth brushed her fingers over them and felt the tingling in her body spreading out along every nerve.

She climbed over him, rocked against his body. He wrapped his arms around her waist and kissed the skin between her breasts. Underneath her, Elizabeth could feel very slight vibration in Ethan's legs. She grabbed his hair in her hands and more violently pushed their bodies together.

He got her earlobe in his teeth and tugged on it, sending shivers through her spine. The rickety dorm bed was bumping against the wall in time, flaking bits of paint from the concrete.

She had to cry out from the pleasure. Like plunging into water, ripples of sensation pressed against her. He began to moan with her. He sat up, his arms tight around her waist and the angle was exactly right to rub her into an oblivion of joy. They orgasmed together and then Ethan flopped back and Elizabeth fell against his sweaty chest with him still inside her. Her cheek was damp and her hair stuck to the edges of her face.

"Oh, Ethan," she said. "That was incredible."

He started laughing and she pulled her head back to look at him. "It rather was, wasn't it?" he said, squeezing her shoulders. She rolled off him and sighed. They fell asleep together that night, still naked and pressed tight against each other on the narrow bed.

She kissed his lips in the morning, but he didn't wake all the way up. She smiled and grabbed her sweater. She left a note for Ethan: "I have my key, so lock the door on your way out." She went to the photo lab to check on her pictures for the school project.

She smiled to herself each time she thought of their bodies pressed together, rocking in rhythm. She didn't know how to keep her focus. The fuzziness around her thoughts was exactly why dating was a bad idea. It was so difficult to concentrate when her mind only wanted to replay all the glory of the previous night. On the other hand, she felt inspired and full of hope and vitality. She took her camera outside to capture images that made her think of hope.

By the time two days went by without a word from Ethan she began to get a sinking feeling in her gut. She felt embarrassed to think of how carefree she had been with her body. It was shaping itself into exactly the same pattern as always. What was wrong with her? Why did men want to never see her again and leave no explanation? Part of her tried to hang onto the thread of hope that Ethan would still reappear, but she was too primed for disappointment now. After a week went by, in her heart she knew that he didn't plan to contact her again.

Ethan didn't seem like the type to disappear. He struck her as a nice, sweet guy. What had happened? Elizabeth was tired of not knowing, of being nice and understanding when men vanished. She went to his dorm and pushed open the door without knocking. Ethan was at his desk, and pulled back suddenly when Elizabeth burst in.

"What is your problem?" she said.

"My problem? What are you doing here?"

"I want to know where you get off disappearing on me. What the hell?"

He looked at her, frowned, looked down at his desk. He pressed his hands against the plywood.

Then he said, "I just thought you're pretty, and able-bodied, and smart. I figured you would be fine, but I have to be careful of my heart. It's easier for me to be hurt." He looked back up at her, his eyes apologetic. Elizabeth was too angry to be softened by his face.

"Do you really believe that? You think because I'm able-bodied, I don't hurt? That I can brush off disappointment easier? You think having a fetish is fun? That I'm like this for my own amusement? You have no fucking idea how badly I've been hurt, how hopeless my life feels."

Had the other men thought this? Had they decided that because she wasn't' disabled she didn't have pain? What self-absorbed jerks. Before Ethan could respond, Elizabeth continued, "I've had enough pain. It was a mistake to try this again. I never should have agreed to go out with you."

"Elizabeth--"

"No. Don't even talk to me. Goddamn men, all you can think about is yourselves. I am so done."

Elizabeth pushed out of his room and jogged down the hallway, trying to get away before she started crying. Why had she thought this man would be different?

On her walk back to her room, Elizabeth tried to mentally pack her feelings back up again. She had done it before. She had spent just a few weeks with her emotions carefully and solidly placed in storage and she had foolishly compromised for a cute boy, but she could get herself locked down for good.

Chapter Ten

"Hey, darlin', who are you here with?"

Elizabeth blushed and looked away. She had three cameras on straps around her neck. "I'm just taking pictures," she said.

She maneuvered into the gym around men transferring from everyday chairs into sports chairs. In front of the bleachers there were several guys and a few girls in graceful wheelchairs waiting for games to start, but the seats behind them were mostly empty.

Elizabeth had been a little afraid to show up here, as though people would just look at her and know she was a sexual deviant. What if someone asked? What if someone accused her of being a dev and everyone was horrified and they kicked her out? She took a deep breath and calmed herself. She had a reason to be here. She put her hand on the cameras. She would keep her answer simple.

There were only a handful of young guys there and they were brash, outgoing jocks. She didn't have the skill or the confidence to just start flirting with them. She was not here to meet a man, anyway. Men were never going to treat her well and it was not worth the headache. She was here to make a difference, to use her talents to benefit the cause she cared most about.

Every once in a while she would mourn her dream, but she had come to a workable peace. She realized that some people were meant for happiness and others weren't. She could still get a lot of satisfaction from doing what she could to help other people find happiness.

The smattering of people in the stands seemed to be wives and husbands of some of the players. Either wheelchair basketball was not a huge draw or their advertising was very poor. Probably both. Elizabeth sat down on the first level of the bleachers, just behind the piles of wheelchairs, sweatshirts, and water bottles.

"When do things get started?" she asked a middle-aged man with no legs sitting next to her. He had a wide, ruddy face and a naturally friendly appearance like her high school chemistry teacher.

"One of the teams hasn't arrived yet," he said. While they waited, Elizabeth chatted with him about his training schedule, how the teams were put together, what made wheelchair basketball different from standard basketball, and a little bit about his three-year-old daughter and how proud he was of her.

Once the games got started, Elizabeth was riveted. She had never before cared so much about a sports game. She hadn't realized how exciting they could be. As players flew down the court, gliding on perfectly aerodynamic wheels, there was a rush of excitement through her gut. She watched the whole thing through her viewfinder, snapping pictures of tangles of players, of clever blocks, of long shots with the basketball soaring through the air, swishing into a basket much higher than it was for most basketball players.

Could she capture images of this fierce game that would show the power of the athletes? Could she show people a photograph of a wheelchair athlete that didn't trigger the "aw, poor him" response? Could she find a way to show this in a way that people would look at these pictures the same as the other sports pictures the paper put out?

At the school newspaper office, Elizabeth held a manila envelope of photos and negatives in her hand and thrust it in front of her to punctuate her words. "Do not put some crap inspirational story with these! People are people. They are not heroes, they are not fodder for inspiration. Treat them the same as any other athlete, not some feel-good sob story."

"I'm sorry, Elizabeth, but you don't have control over what story these go with. Once you sell us the pictures, we can use them however we want."

"'Inspiration' is what's wrong with the world," she muttered.

She wasn't surprised when she picked up the paper the next week and found the article dripping with pretentious cliches. The men enjoying an athletic outlet the same as many others would became special people defying the odds and doing what they loved in spite of their disabilities.

Two girls came up and opened the paper while Elizabeth was still standing there. "Aw, isn't that sweet? Good on them for putting in an effort," one of them said.

"I know!" The other replied, "Not many would keep trying. Even though it's not the same, it's so good they can try."

"Excuse me," Elizabeth said, "Would you ever go to a wheelchair sporting event?"

Both girls turned to her and frowned. "No," one said. "Why would I?"

"It's a very exciting game; they're real athletes," Elizabeth said.

They giggled. "It's cute and all that they want to pretend to play sports; I mean, really good on them and thank goodness for those brave people who run programs for these poor guys, but I don't want to actually watch it," one of them said. She put down her copy of the paper and walked away.

Elizabeth bought ten copies, even as she grumbled to herself about people's incredible ignorance and prejudice. The pictures were some of her very best work and she wanted them for her portfolio.

The dorm phone was ringing when Elizabeth came back from class. She ran for it and was not surprised that it was her mother. "We're coming to pick you up," Susan said. "Libby just had her baby."

"Oh my God!"

"Yes, so we're going to see them at the hospital."

"Great. I'll meet you out front." Elizabeth packed a purse and some school supplies and ran out the door. She felt a similar twisting in her stomach that she had felt when she went to Libby's wedding last year. Was her cousin really old enough to be doing these things? To be having this life? A baby. It was too surreal.

Libby and her parents and husband were all in the room when they arrived. The baby was sleeping in a plastic basin with a mattress. "Go and see," Susan urged. Elizabeth crept close to it and looked at the tiny baby girl.

"You can hold her when she wakes up," Libby said.

"Oh," Elizabeth said, "I don't know."

A few minutes later, though, she was being shuffled to a hard little sofa and the baby was pressed into her arms. She looked down at it and it looked up at her. They just stared at each other for a long time.

This new life was so beautiful. There was a freshness to the wrinkled, blinking creature, who did not understand anything that she was seeing, as fascinated by the lights as Susan's earrings or Elizabeth's golden hair.

Gazing down at the infant, Elizabeth couldn't help wondering what strange longings this girl would grow up to have. How soon would she be aware of her sexuality? In what ways would this girl hurt her mother the way Elizabeth hurt Susan?

Elizabeth was struck with a brief understanding: she had once been small and helpless like this. No wonder Susan still hovered. She had looked at Elizabeth and saw a tiny, hopeful, innocent creature. No way for her to know how it would turn out, that her perfect little baby would grow into a life of struggling to be at peace with her own heart.

Elizabeth did not want to disappoint the hopeful young mother that Susan had once been. If Elizabeth couldn't be the daughter she had expected and wanted, would Susan regret ever having her at all? When Elizabeth insisted on following her desires in dating and going against what her mother wanted, was she causing Susan to wish that she had never had a child? Or maybe she would just wish that she had a different child. What if she wished it had been Elizabeth who died in the womb and that she had a son? A simple and easy son who would go to law school and meet a pretty brunette his second year, marry her at the end of school and settle into a grand house a couple of miles from Susan and David. Wasn't that the scenario Susan envisioned when she was pregnant with Elizabeth?

Then Robert and the rest of his family arrived. Libby's husband was his brother and Elizabeth hadn't thought about the possibility of seeing him here. She handed the baby over to his mother and hung out on the other side of the room while Robert congratulated his brother and Libby. They didn't say anything to each other. Even though he probably wasn't thinking or caring about her at all, Elizabeth still felt embarrassed around him. What if he was quietly gloating that she and Stewart were no longer together? He won in a way. Elizabeth scolded herself. This was such a self-centered way to think. Robert was just there to see the baby; he didn't care that Elizabeth wasn't dating his best friend anymore.

After the hospital, Elizabeth went home with her parents. She had a photo shoot set up for her project that was closer to their place. Elizabeth had brought home the binder where she saved copies of all her best work. It was a large binder with plastic sheets to hold the pictures, but so far there were only a few actual photos in it. The first was the photo she had taken of Stewart that got into a magazine last year. Next were a few for class assignments. Also, the wheelchair basketball pictures she had given to the school newspaper. There were also a few of the early picks for her semester project. She planned to work on organizing them while she was home.

The next morning Elizabeth woke in her old bedroom still feeling the strange awe of seeing her mother in a new way. Susan had been young like Libby when Elizabeth was born. She had probably been as confused and uncertain and startled by the baby she was suddenly responsible for. It was a new kind of guilt that began tugging at Elizabeth. She resolved to try to go easier on her mother.

First, though, she was going to be taking pictures of children at a daycare for special needs kids. In exchange for using some of the pictures for school she was going to give the parents free copies. Walking into the daycare immediately put Elizabeth at ease. The bright yellow walls and posters of balloons and rainbows really did make her smile. Elizabeth chatted with the woman who owned the company for a few minutes, then she set up a station and brought kids over. She took pictures of them playing together and pictures of them separately. She stayed until lunchtime taking pictures. She couldn't remember the last time she had so much fun. There was nothing like spending time with kids to raise your spirits. It was nice to see children of all different abilities playing together. The kids all loved posing too and were anxious to get in as many pictures as possible. Elizabeth used her digital camera so she could show them their images immediately.

"Thanks, Elizabeth," the owner said, giving her a stack of release slips from the parents. "This was a fun change of pace for them."

"I had a great time," she said. "I'm going to get nice prints of all these pictures and I'll mail them to you so you can distribute to the parents."

"Sounds great. Thanks for coming."

Elizabeth couldn't help wondering what would have happened if the owner knew that she was a fetishist. Not that she was getting turned on by little kids at all, but people didn't really seem to understand that distinction. She suspected that the same woman who was so friendly and grateful to her would call the police if she knew that one detail about Elizabeth.

When she got home, Elizabeth opened the door to her room to find Susan there. Her stomach seized up. These days she was always afraid of what her mother was going to say. Susan was facing her bed where the binder of photos was open.

"Mom? What are you doing?"

Susan grabbed a handful of the pictures that Elizabeth had been organizing and turned with them in her hand. "What is this?" she said.

"My photographs," Elizabeth said. "My school work."

"This obsession has gone far enough," Susan said, and there was a dangerous glow in her eyes that Elizabeth had not seen before. Susan scooped up all the photos and walked out of the room. Elizabeth followed her, frowning, not knowing what her mother was doing. Susan went to the kitchen and pulled out the trashcan from under the sink. One by one she began to tear the pictures to pieces and let the bits flutter into the trash. Elizabeth's eyes widened. She was so startled that she couldn't move. Her own mother was destroying her work; it was too surreal to believe. At least these weren't the negatives. Elizabeth was glad she had left those at her dorm.

Susan finished making confetti out of Elizabeth's photographs and walked back out of the kitchen, past

Elizabeth without looking at her. Elizabeth followed her when she felt able to move again.

"My pictures help people," she said to her mother's back.

"No," Susan said, "your pictures are pieces of paper and they aren't doing anyone any good. This is not open for discussion."

"You're wrong."

"Enough. We are done."

Elizabeth tried to say something, but she could feel tears rising in her, so she just shrugged and ran up the stairs to her room, closing the door behind her.

Those pictures represented her entire future. What was she going to do if her mother wouldn't let her express devness even in this way? Elizabeth curled up on her bed under the cover. Every time she closed her eyes she could see her precious pictures being torn to bits. This house felt like a prison. Everything weighed on her more when she was here.

In the morning, Elizabeth was scared to get out of bed. She sat in the center, her arms wrapped around her legs, and wondered what Susan was going to be like. Guilt prickled at her stomach as she thought again of Libby's perfect little baby. Elizabeth's resolution to be nicer to her mother had failed already.

Coming down the stairs, she could see the back of Susan's head, her blonde hair wound tightly into a French twist, as her mother sat quietly on the sofa. No television was on and Susan wasn't reading anything, she was just sitting.

"Mom?" Elizabeth said.

Susan turned and looked at her. The expression on her face was sad, and there was defeat in it. Elizabeth hadn't wanted to cause this.

"I just don't understand what goes on in your head, Elizabeth," Susan said.

Elizabeth bit her lip.

Susan continued, looking blankly at the dark rug and not at her daughter. "Deciding that you have to be with a handicapped man. It's just not normal."

Elizabeth sat down on a chair beside the couch. Her mother still didn't look at her, but Elizabeth felt as though she could see the gears turning in Susan's head as she tried so hard to understand where Elizabeth was coming from. She was making an effort. She really was trying.

"I don't know what I did wrong," Susan said. "What happened to you while I wasn't looking? I should never have been a working mother."

"It's not your fault," Elizabeth said. "This is about me, not you."

Finally Susan raised her eyes to Elizabeth and the sadness was palpable. "But I'm your mother," she said. "I shaped you. I taught you. Everything you are is because of me."

"That's not true," Elizabeth insisted. "You don't believe in a blank slate. You told me yourself that I came into the world with a personality. This is my stuff to work out." She paused, then said something that felt to her like admitting defeat. "Maybe I could see a therapist about this thing?"

Susan nodded slowly. "I think that's a good idea, Elizabeth."

Elizabeth herself wasn't so sure, but she would do almost anything to make her mother feel better.

Elizabeth went back to school, but by the next weekend Susan had an appointment set up for her. Her mother picked her up Friday afternoon and drove her to an unfamiliar part of Arlington. They didn't say much to each other. Elizabeth felt that her mother was more relaxed, though, happy that Elizabeth was going along with this plan to get to the root of her sexuality and yank it out. At this point Elizabeth couldn't help thinking it was a good plan. The strain of bad dates had worn her down. Why shouldn't she find a way to broaden her horizons?

"This is it," Susan said as they arrived at a short brick building. "I'll go in with you." She parked and they got out, walking up to the building with Elizabeth lagging behind. Inside there were several offices. Susan found the right number and knocked. She turned to Elizabeth, and squeezed her shoulder. "Make me proud," Susan said.

"Come in," a voice said and Elizabeth pushed the door, slipping in. While it closed behind her, Elizabeth paused to take in the room. It didn't look like she imagined a therapist's office. Rather it was cozy feeling, with a large window and lace curtains, three big cushion chairs in white fabric and a gathering of plants in one corner.

"Welcome," the woman in the room said. She was younger than Susan and her clothes were more flowy and relaxed. "Have a seat wherever you like."

Elizabeth bit her lip and nodded, dropping onto one of the white chairs. The woman sat in another. "I'm Ramona," she said. She had pulled out a clipboard with paper and a pen. "Tell me what brings you here today, Elizabeth."

Elizabeth twisted her hands in her lap for a moment, then answered. "I have this thing. And I don't know where it came from."

Ramona hadn't written anything on the paper. She leaned forward and said in a soft voice, "What kind of thing?"

"A sexual thing," Elizabeth said, feeling as though she might choke on the word "sexual."

"Can you tell me more about it?" Ramona prompted her.

Elizabeth looked away, down at the flowered carpet. "Didn't my mom say? On the phone?"

"I'd like to hear you tell me about it." Her voice continued to be soft and gentle, not changing pitch.

"I'm only attracted to men who are physically disabled," Elizabeth said. She had started getting used to this statement. She'd said it to dates and on the internet. It seemed to capture the important core of what devness was, though it was considerably simplified.

"That's very unusual," Ramona said.

"Yeah," Elizabeth acknowledged.

"And you came here today for what reason? To change it?"

Elizabeth slid her hands under her thighs and looked around as though Susan could be lurking somewhere in the room. "I don't know," she said. "I don't know that it can be changed."

"If it could, would you do that?"

"Maybe," Elizabeth said. She had expected to be more certain that she would do whatever she had to to get rid of it. Yet she found that there was some affection for the devness, some attachment and fear of it leaving. "Some days," she said, "I would do anything for it to go away. Other days I'm so grateful it's there."

"How so?"

"It's always been a part of me. It's been something I turn to again and again. I don't know who I would be without it. I don't know if I'd ever feel attraction like I do now again. They say that women don't get an instant attraction. But I do. I like having that."

"Okay," Ramona said, now writing on the clipboard. "That sounds reasonable. Tell me, though, Elizabeth. Do you feel happy?"

Elizabeth swallowed. "If I did, I wouldn't be here."

"Good insight," Ramona said. "What I want for you is happiness. Whatever form that takes. Whether it means trying to change your sexual desire or whether it means managing it in your life."

"You're not going to try to cure me?"

"Not necessarily."

"You didn't say that to my mother, did you?"

"No. What we do here is for you, not for her."

After the session Elizabeth sat outside waiting for Susan to pick her up and wondered how therapy was going to do anything for her. Just talking wasn't really any different from what she had already done. She had Amy to talk to. She had Stewart. Even if it didn't do anything, though, it would make Susan happy if Elizabeth kept going, so she would.

On the ride home, Susan said, "So what did you say about me?"

"Nothing," Elizabeth muttered.

"Did you tell her what a bad mother I've been?"

"Mom, come on. You're not a bad mother. It isn't about you."

"How can it not be?" She was focused on the road and did not turn her glance to Elizabeth at all. Even though Susan always wanted a response, Elizabeth didn't say anything. There was nothing to say. She couldn't tell Susan that the therapist had not called devness evil.

Since she was already at home she decided to stay for the weekend. Weekends on campus were becoming depressing. She didn't have Cassie to talk to and she didn't want to accidentally run into Ethan after yelling at him.

That night, playing on the internet on the family computer in the den, she saw something that she didn't intend to. She was careful to avoid looking for information about other devotees. She had been too scarred by what she'd found when she first found out about the word. She still looked up information about disability rights, though. She looked for ways that she could use her photography to further the cause. It was an accident that she saw someone's message about devotees. *Watch out for those lowlife creeps. What kind of a sick world do we live in that people like this exist?*

Elizabeth leapt back and jumped up as her chair crashed to the floor. Tears pressed against her eyes. It was like walking into a room and overhearing people saying nasty things about you. There was nowhere for her to hide from the terrible feelings that rushed in.

"Elizabeth? What's going on?" Susan's voice called from the kitchen.

"Nothing," Elizabeth choked out. She shut down the computer and ran out of the room, taking the stairs to her room two at a time. With the door closed, she sank to the ground, her cheek pressed on hardwood. *Fine*, she thought, *you win. You hate me, you never met me but you hate me. I give up. I want to cease to exist.* All those people on the internet who expressed disgust at devotees hated her even though they didn't know her. She didn't have the energy to fight them.

The feeling settled deep in her gut, the knowledge that there was no one out there for her. It was all a lie. No one was coming. No one was coming for her, no one to make her feel better or to be her hero. She wanted to fade out of existence. Not to die, but to be replaced by a better her. A better daughter and friend, one who didn't carry these dark thoughts. She felt all the energy draining out of her. There was no desire to move, no desire to engage in life.

Hate pooled in her. She hated herself. Her hope was leaking away and taking any joy or faith in humanity with it. She felt as though she were unraveling at the seams, and in fact, she had been for years. She had tried to hold herself together and now she was just too threadbare not to burst. She was sinking and the farther she sank, the farther she was from love, the one thing she desired. *It is not coming for you. You are alone.* That voice she hadn't heard in months was suddenly back. It had never gone away, just waited until Elizabeth would be weak enough to listen again. It rubbed at her and she was sure it would keep rubbing until there was nothing left, sandpaper on her flesh.

What was there to be so unhappy about? Her mind longed to share itself, to share all the love that she was capable of, and it was finding no outlet. *I have nothing to give*, she thought, *I take up space and energy draining those around me.* Now all she wanted was to stop hurting them and herself, just stop the pain.

She didn't believe in suicide. She knew it wouldn't be fair to her parents or friends to make them suffer through her death. So she didn't want to die so much as to never have existed at all. She wanted to just fade away into nothing and have no more pain. No more people thinking these awful things about her. No weight of bad vibes against her. These people made her feel that she had no right to exist, no good in her, no reason to go on trying to find happiness.

She felt so tired. So unbearably tired of the effort of life. It was too much, she couldn't do it. She wasn't strong enough and she was more than ready to give up. These people were calling for her blood. And she hadn't ever hurt anyone. *If you killed yourself, they'd be happy. They just want a world without people like you.*

Chapter Eleven

The alarm clock went off and Elizabeth woke, still on the floor. There was a puddle of drool under her cheek on the hardwood and her eyes were crusted shut with dried tears.

She stood up slowly and her bones cracked. She looked at her door and just couldn't face going out. Her mother would be there waiting with an I-told-you-so smirk. In a stack of school books, Elizabeth's eye fell on the copy of *Frankenstein*. She felt like the monster at this moment.

Stumbling into bed, she pulled the covers over her head and fell into a light and feverish sleep. Time slipped by and Elizabeth was not aware of it. Occasionally she went into the bathroom, but quickly returned to her bed. She didn't feel any hunger or anything besides an overwhelming desire to sleep. While she slept she didn't have to think about any of it. It was the closest she could get to not existing.

Days must have gone by because Susan came in one morning and said, "Aren't you going to school?"

Elizabeth didn't respond. She felt as though she couldn't. Couldn't move, couldn't speak. There was a heavy burden on her and she couldn't push it off.

"I'm taking you back to that therapist. Come on, put on a coat."

Susan took hold of her elbow and pulled her out of bed, put a coat over her and dragged her to the car. Elizabeth didn't protest. When they got to the therapist's office, Susan gave Elizabeth a little push in the door. Elizabeth fell onto one of the white chairs without looking at Ramona.

"What's wrong, Elizabeth?"

Tears spilled down her cheeks suddenly. "There's so much hatred," she whispered. "I don't want to be hated. It is evil, isn't it?"

"No. I don't think so. Let's talk about it a little more and see what we can uncover. Okay?"

Elizabeth nodded.

"Are you afraid of men?"

"No," Elizabeth said, "I don't think so. But it's like asking me to want to have sex with other girls. I just don't have the desire."

"And with disabled men you do?"

"Yes." She looked down at her fingers.

"But they are still men."

"I know. I'm not sure what makes them different."

"Perhaps there was some incident that could have caused this? Can you remember any experience with a disabled person when you were a child?"

Elizabeth felt something snapping inside her. "You people always want a reason to point so you can dismiss it as nothing more than a moment of trauma," she said, almost shouting. "Because that keeps you safe. If you can pin down a reason, then you can prevent it in your kids. Then you can say, 'Oh thank God, there's a reason.' But it's so much more complicated than that. This was not one experience that wired me wrong forever."

"I see."

"And to answer your question, no. There was no particular experience with anyone who had a disability in my childhood."

"I don't want to tell you this is wrong, Elizabeth. What concerns me is the addictive quality of what you describe. I don't think we need to make it go away, but it would be good if you felt in control of it, not a slave to it."

Elizabeth nodded. The outburst made her feel better. It had cleared her mind a little and she thought she could see her way through to a life where devness was balanced. "I can live with trying to do that," she said. "I've tried to make devness go away in the past and it never does. It might dial down for a while, but it always comes back."

The therapist nodded. "I think you know deep inside you that you're okay. You're feeling uncertain because your feeling of what's right and your mother's are so different. Trust yourself."

"Do you think you could tell my mom that it's not her fault?" Elizabeth said. "That wherever it came from, it wasn't something that she did to me."

"I think you need to talk to her," Ramona said.

Elizabeth swallowed. "You're right," she said.

When Susan came to pick her up, Elizabeth got in the car and wondered how she could talk to her mother about this. Susan said, "Feel better now?"

"Yeah," Elizabeth said. Then she decided that the only thing to do was to jump right in and stop trying to put off talking to Susan about her sexuality. "Mom, listen. Stewart wasn't an anomaly. He won't be the last man in a wheelchair that I date."

Elizabeth saw Susan's fingers grip the steering wheel more tightly. "Don't make rash decisions, Elizabeth. I know this is some kind of boundary testing, but it's exhausting me."

"You? It's exhausting you? How many times do I have to tell you that this isn't about you?"

"Of course it is. Maybe I should have forced you to play more with other children. Maybe I should have monitored what you were reading."

"It's just something that I have. It's called devoteeism."

"You don't have to corner yourself like this. You're so young, just keep an open mind and don't limit yourself with labels."

"I've been living with this for nineteen years."

Susan drew in a deep breath. "So have we," she said. "So have we."

"It's not your fault, Mom. It's not your fault and it's not mine, it's just something that is. And I can't live my life without it."

"I will do whatever it takes to fix this. You have got to work with me, though. I'm thinking about what's best for you."

"For me? Really? Or are you just afraid that people will think me having a fetish is because you were a bad mother?"

"Elizabeth! Enough."

"No, it's not enough. I can't spend my whole life trying to make you happy. What you're asking of me is more than I can give. I won't sacrifice myself forever. What are you expecting? For me to just stay here with you forever? Is that what you want?"

"Of course not. I want you to let go of this silliness and date a normal man."

Elizabeth decided to skip over the philosophical debate of what being normal even meant. "I know you can't understand it, but couldn't you please trust me that it isn't possible?"

"The therapy isn't working, is it?"

"Maybe it is. Maybe it's making me more sure of myself."

"That's not why we brought you there."

"I know. But it's what I needed."

They rode the rest of the way in terse silence. Elizabeth felt energized by finally standing up to her mother, though. While she was on the high she decided to find out if her father really felt the same way as Susan about these things. Her mother would have her believe that both her parents had a completely united view on this, but her father never spoke about it. He had stuck up for her so many times in the past, if anyone could find the words to make Susan understand, he could.

Elizabeth found David alone in his study.

"Daddy?"

David looked over at her. His expression didn't change and Elizabeth couldn't read it. She came in and sat down on his sofa. Even though they had never talked about it, Elizabeth stopped filtering herself. "Do you really believe that I should be with someone I hate having sex with?"

As uncomfortable as he looked, Elizabeth didn't say anything to put him at ease. He coughed, brushed the side of his eyebrow with his hand, and said to his desk, "Girls don't really need it the same way. You can just close your eyes and think of something else." He paused, glanced at her briefly and added, "Lots of women do that."

Tears leaked out of the sides of Elizabeth's eyes, hot against her cheek and dropping onto her hand. She couldn't bring herself to tell her father that she loved sex, that the thought of lying back and thinking of England for the rest of her life made her want to end it now. She felt as though she were suffocating. Was that what lots of women did? Was that what her mother did? Closed her eyes and thought of something else every single night?

All this time she thought she deserved a relationship of equal partnership with someone she was attracted to. Maybe only a very few select people actually achieved that. Elizabeth shivered, her arms suddenly breaking out in goosebumps. If this was adulthood, it was not what she had signed up for. It was the first time she really considered her parents' expectations and disappointments. It was like they were trying to induct her into a secret society and she just could not accept the rules.

Chapter Twelve

Back at school, Elizabeth reorganized her pictures. She added in the images from the daycare, blending them with all the others. Flipping through it, she felt a bittersweet pride. As much as she loved her work, each time she looked at her pictures she remembered her mother tearing them up and throwing them away.

After submitting the final portfolio, Elizabeth went back to her room and studied for a Chemistry test. She lay on her bed on her stomach, highlighting her textbook and swinging her legs in the air when there was a knock on her door. She stuck the highlighter in the spine of the book and bounced up. Looking through the peephole she saw Ethan's dark brown eyes.

She was too surprised to move and just stood there for several minutes, still looking out the peephole. She watched as Ethan shifted his weight onto his left crutch, then knocked again with his right hand. Still Elizabeth couldn't quite bring herself to open the door. She just kept standing there with her eye against the door. Outside Ethan sighed and Elizabeth licked her lips as he maneuvered himself around to leave. She slowly pulled open the door.

"Wait," she said.

He stopped, but didn't turn. Elizabeth looked at the sexy way he leaned forward on the crutches.

"Why don't you come around to this side of me?" he said.

"Depends what you're here for," she said to the back of his head.

"I'm sorry," Ethan said.

Elizabeth walked around him, stepping carefully over one crutch, and passing so closely to him that she could smell his skin. He bit his lip and looked at the floor.

"You were right," he continued. "I think you're a great girl. It's hard for me to trust that you could possibly be interested in me."

"Right. So that's why you decided to hurt my feelings."

"I wasn't thinking. The point is, I'm here now. I'm swallowing my pride and I'm saying I'm sorry."

"Okay. And you're looking for me to forgive you?"

"Well, yeah. And maybe more than that." He raised his eyes and met hers, gave a small smile. "Can we start over?"

"I don't know," Elizabeth said. She frowned, wanting so much to just forget what he had done. "How do I know it will be different?"

"Just give me a chance."

These last weeks of feeling rejected, of feeling hopeless, of letting her mother take her to therapy, could she forgive all that? His eyes were sad and she liked that he wasn't holding back. She could see his emotions in his face, unlike with Stewart. Finally, she reached out and touched the side of his face, feeling the light layer of stubble over his skin. "You're just too cute," she said. "I'll tell you what; you tell me something that makes you vulnerable. Then I'll forgive you."

Ethan smiled. "All right," he said. "Can we go into your room first? So I don't have to vulnerable in the hallway?"

Elizabeth nodded. She went back to her bed and Ethan followed. While she sat, he stood, leaning on his crutches in the way that gave her an urge to grab hold of his body and press it against hers. "Okay," he said, "here goes. You know how I told you that my dad left when I was a baby?"

Elizabeth nodded.

"It was because of me. Because of my disability."

"Oh my God." This was a bigger revelation than she had expected.

"Yeah," Ethan said. "He couldn't deal with having a messed-up kid. All those pity posters in the grocery store; he didn't want that to be his family."

"I'm so sorry," Elizabeth said.

"Is that vulnerable enough for you?" he said.

She nodded and patted the bed beside her. He pulled his arms out of the crutches and stumbled onto the bed. "Promise me this," Elizabeth said, "from now on we talk about these things."

Ethan smirked. "Talk? You want to talk?"

"Well, maybe not at this particular moment." She put her arms around his neck and kissed him.

This time when they made love it was more gentle and sweet. Ethan touched the side of her face while she was naked, leaning close over him. He brushed his fingers through her wavy hair. The air in the room became hot and stuffy. Elizabeth felt like they were building the friction and energy slowly into her room. She savored him, breathing deeply of his pine-tree scent and pressing her face into the crook of his neck.

Afterward, lying side by side on the narrow bed, his arm under her head, Ethan said, "So are you my girlfriend now?"

"Do you want me to be?"

Ethan turned to look at her. "Yeah," he said, "I do."

"Okay then," Elizabeth said, smacking his shoulder with the back of her hand.

"I'm not going to be banging you against a bathroom wall or anything like that."

Elizabeth turned her head, propped herself up on an elbow, and raised an eyebrow at him.

"I just want to clarify. Don't know what your expectations are," he said.

Elizabeth shook her head. "It's cute how insecure you are."

"What? I'm just realistic."

"I have never wanted to be banged against a bathroom wall, thanks."

"Well, when you put it like that it doesn't sound good."

"I put it exactly how you put it!"

"I mean like in the movies; it always looks urgent and sexy."

"If you're basing what you expect life to be like on movies than I have some bad news for you."

He smiled and she lay her head back down so she could feel his curls against her own forehead.

"How is the project going?" he asked.

"Good. I've submitted it for review, so now I'm just waiting to hear back if it makes it to the gallery."

"I bet you'll get it."

"Only one project gets picked from all the sections of Photography 230."

"You have a great project."

Elizabeth laughed. "Thanks for the confidence," she said, "but you never saw it finished."

Ethan didn't join her laughter. "Why don't you show it to me now?" he said.

"Yeah?"

"Yeah."

"All right," Elizabeth said. She felt a warm glow of pride as she went to her desk and pulled out her portfolio with all the images for the assignment. This was her backup copy. Side by side, she and Ethan flipped through the pages and he made appreciative sounds. He was able to comment on her abilities as a photographer and she liked getting his input on her composition.

Ethan slept over that night. In the dark room, early in the morning, Elizabeth opened her eyes, surprised to find herself awake. Ethan's body was pressed against her back and his arm was around her waist. She didn't move, but just looked at his crutches propped against her desk and smiled.

Then his voice, soft and gravely with sleep, whispered, "Are you awake?"

"Yes," she said without moving. His arm tightened around her and she lay her hand over his.

"Are you okay?" he said. "I mean, really."

Elizabeth almost brushed off the question, but the stillness of the quiet morning felt too honest. "I don't know," she said. "I went to see a therapist."

"What for?"

"To cure me, I guess."

Ethan pulled her body until she was facing him. He touched the side of her face gently. "There's nothing wrong with you," he said.

Elizabeth gave a small smile. "I hope someday I believe that," she said.

He kissed her forehead, then pulled her closer and closed his eyes. Elizabeth closed her eyes too and soon drifted back to sleep.

In the morning they decided to get breakfast at the cafeteria. "I'm going to be doing the walk of shame," Ethan said with a smile. "Wearing the same clothes."

"Eh," Elizabeth said, "guy clothes all look alike."

Ethan kissed her cheek. "I'm pretty sure it's a walk of awesome when it's a guy anyway."

He walked into the hallway and Elizabeth locked her door. While she was putting her keys in her pocket, the door across the hall opened and Cassie stared at them. Elizabeth's smile fell off her face quickly. Cassie's eyes were wide, her mouth a little bit ajar.

"Hey," Ethan said in a friendly tone. Elizabeth hadn't told him about her hall mate.

"Hello, how are you?" she said loudly and slowly at Ethan and he and Elizabeth exchanged confused glances.

"Cassie?" Elizabeth said. "What are you doing?"

Cassie very slowly turned her gaze to Elizabeth and the fury in her eyes was almost like a physical slap. Elizabeth stepped back and bumped into the wall.

"You should be ashamed of yourself," Cassie hissed and disappeared back into her room.

"What was that all about?" Elizabeth asked as she walked behind Ethan towards the door.

"She thinks I'm mentally challenged."

"What? That's crazy."

Ethan shrugged. "Yeah. People are crazy. It happens to me a lot."

Elizabeth thought about that. Ethan's speech was affected a little bit by the CP. His words struggled out of his mouth. Perhaps that gave people the impression that he was mentally slower.

"For a lot of people, weird movement has to mean mental impairment," Ethan said. "They just don't know any better. All the images they've ever seen of crutches like mine or a walk like mine are connected to retardation."

Outside, they walked side by side towards the cafeteria. "People are idiots," Elizabeth said. "Cassie has such a problem with me, but it's not like I'm having sex with people who have brain damage or something."

"Actually, you kind of are," Ethan said, grinning at her.

"Oh. Right. Thanks, that's really helping."

"Brain damage that doesn't affect mental capacity, though," Ethan said. "So it's okay."

"You do know how to make a girl feel better."

After breakfast, Ethan went to a class and Elizabeth returned to her room. Sitting on the bed, she reflected on how strange life was. Things never happened the way she expected them to. Whenever she thought she knew what path she was on, some twist came along to throw her off. She had not expected to see Ethan again.

She had to tell someone the good news that he was back. She pulled out her cell phone and called Stewart.

"Hey, Elizabeth," he said, his voice upbeat. "How are you?"

"I'm good," she said. She bit her lip, then burst out, "I started seeing someone."

"That's great," Stewart said. "Disabled guy?"

"Yeah."

"I'm really glad."

"Thanks. I think he's jealous of you."

Stewart laughed and it made Elizabeth smile. She said, "You're an intimidating guy to live up to. You're back in magazines, eh?"

"Yep. Crip of the year, that's me. However people want to see me is fine. I'm just following what feels right."

"That's not always easy to do."

"Your mom still giving you grief?"

"I'm afraid of what she'll do when she finds out about Ethan. You don't think she'll cut me off, do you?"

"I don't know. I'm sorry; I wish I could tell you something nicer. I only met her that one time and I think if she could have killed me with her eyes, she would have."

Elizabeth sighed. "I just don't know how to keep everyone happy."

"That's your problem. You can't. Worry about your own happiness and let your mom worry about hers. It's not your job."

"Easy to say, not easy to do."

"I know. But don't start thinking about her. You've got someone that you like. Focus on that."

"Okay," Elizabeth said. "Thanks."

"Anytime."

Elizabeth continued to see Ethan. They spent every night together in one of their rooms. Most days they met up for lunch at the cafeteria and traded notes on camera techniques. The next time Susan called, Elizabeth didn't answer. She just looked at the name flashing on her cell phone and let it go to voice mail. She wasn't ready to tell Susan about her new boyfriend and she was afraid that if she answered, she wouldn't be able to stop herself from mentioning him. They were spending so much time together that everything in her life was now touched by him.

One day when they were having lunch, crowds of people buzzing around them, Ethan said, "Do you want to come home with me this weekend? Meet my mom?"

Elizabeth almost choked on her fries. Meeting his family? Wasn't it too soon for that? But she said, "Sure, yeah, I could do that."

"Cool. We'll take the subway to Braintree and Mom will pick us up there."

Elizabeth had never been all the way to the Braintree stop. Her home was close to the opposite end of the red line, Alewife.

"This weekend, huh?" she said.

He nodded and continued eating, not at all concerned. Elizabeth was pretty sure he wouldn't have told his mother that she had a fetish. Even so, it always felt as though people could tell, like they could just look at her and know. Would his mother be suspicious that Elizabeth was interested in her son? Would she think there must be something wrong? Luckily, there were plenty of other reasons for Elizabeth to be dating him. If asked, she could always talk about how they had photography in common. This was going to be fine.

On Friday afternoon they stood outside the subway entrance with backpacks on enjoying the spring sun. Elizabeth faced Ethan and whispered, "Is it bad that I wish I could have you right here in the street?"

"Not bad at all," Ethan said. He smiled and kissed her. She grabbed the sides of his face and pushed her lips harder against his. The sun was hot on the back of her neck. She stepped closer until she could feel his bent legs trembling against hers and rested her hands on top of his on his crutches.

When Elizabeth stepped back, he was squinting against the sun, his brown curls almost long enough to fall into his eyes.

"Come on," he said, "stop stalling."

Elizabeth sat next to Ethan on the small, narrow seats of the subway. They were pressed together all the way down their bodies. He took her hand and held it.

Here she was going to meet his mother and she hadn't even told her family he existed. This was feeling familiar, just like last year when she had hidden her boyfriend for months. She had promised herself she wouldn't do that again. Keeping Stewart a secret had led to more problems than being honest would have. This time she had to do it differently. She had to tell her parents and be up-front about his having a disability. She promised herself when she got back after this weekend she would tell her parents about her new boyfriend. She would tell them he was disabled but not give it too much emphasis. If they were going to be uncomfortable with another disabled boyfriend, that was not going to be her problem. They just had to learn to deal with it.

At the other end of the subway line they got out of the station and Ethan headed towards a woman standing beside a car. She looked young to Elizabeth, certainly at least ten years younger than her parents, and much more in fashion than her mother. Ethan's mother was wearing jeans and a loose bohemian top with curly black hair loose in the wind. Elizabeth had rarely seen her mother wear anything other than a suit of some kind. Susan's hair was always slicked back into a French twist with no strays.

"Mom, this is Elizabeth," Ethan said when they reached the woman.

"Hello, sweetie, it's good to meet you. I'm Monica."

Elizabeth climbed into the backseat with their backpacks and Ethan got in the front. Elizabeth watched as he backed up to the seat and dropped onto it, pulling his legs in and then laying his crutches beside him. On the ride she half-listened while he and his mother talked about school.

The house, when they arrived, was small and square. It was painted yellow and nestled next to several other houses that looked the same but in different colors. Monica led the way inside and Elizabeth was last in the door.

There were pictures on all the walls, several of them groupings of family photos. Elizabeth had never before thought how odd it was that her family didn't decorate with photographs. There were a couple of paintings on the walls at home, but nothing of much personal significance: generic landscapes or still lives of fruit. The result here was warm and cozy. Elizabeth felt as though she could see a whole life in a glance just by looking at the living room. The furnishings were softer too than at her house. The couch and chairs were fabric with big flower prints and a ruffle along the bottom. An empty vase was placed on an antique-looking doily on a side table. The curtains were a creamy color. At

Elizabeth's the living room floor was dark wood and the furniture was crisp, dark, and clean-lined.

"I've made up a bed for you in the guest room, Elizabeth," Ethan's mother said.

"Oh. Thanks." She shouldn't be surprised that Ethan's mother didn't want them staying in the same room. It still seemed a little strange. She was nineteen and he was twenty. They were off at college without her supervision. If they wanted to have sex, they would. And they did. Giving them separate bedrooms for the weekend was a little like putting her fingers in her ears and humming.

The house was a ranch, so it had only one main floor. There was a basement, of course, and an attic. Ethan took Elizabeth on a tour. She followed behind him and watched his feet brushing each other with every step. At the back of the house was a junk room, and when Elizabeth peeked her head in she saw some small trophies and pictures of wheelchair races.

"Hey," she said, "I thought you said you weren't athletic."

"Yeah," he said, "I tried track when I was a kid and it wasn't my thing."

That night they had dinner on TV tray tables in the living room watching *Jeopardy*. Elizabeth felt comfortable and relaxed. So far she was liking Ethan's mother. There was a real sense of warmth and love in this house.

During commercial breaks, Ethan's mother asked Elizabeth questions.

"What is your family like, Liz?"

"They're good. My dad's a professor and my mom runs an advertising company."

"How do you like school?"

"It's great."

After dinner Ethan's mother went to her room to read and left them to sit in the living room and watch ghost stories on the Discovery channel.

"I like your mom," Elizabeth said. She snuggled up against Ethan on the sofa.

He smiled. "Yeah, she's been great."

Elizabeth took his hand and squeezed it. She admired his unusually long fingers. His hands were long, narrow, and beautiful.

The whole weekend was peaceful and Elizabeth was sorry when it ended. She wished she felt this relaxed around her own family. The first thing she thought when she got back to campus and kissed Ethan goodbye was that she needed to tell her parents about him. It wasn't right to try to hide him to protect herself from having to deal with their objections.

Even if she had never told them about the devness, chances were they would have a problem with him anyway. Elizabeth couldn't imagine what it was like to have your daughter say that she was dating a man who had a severe mobility disability. It had to be strange. Parents must worry about whether the girl was settling, whether she thought she couldn't score a "normal" man. Sometimes Elizabeth thought she could almost see that point of view, but she couldn't quite grasp it. It slipped away just as she got close to it. Her own ideas about disability were just too strong.

After she put her clothes away and showered, Elizabeth called her mother.

"We haven't heard from you in a while," Susan said.

"Yeah," Elizabeth said. She sat on her bed and pulled her knees up to her chest. Even though she wasn't in the same room with Susan, she still felt an instinctive need to protect her body.

"Are you coming home next weekend?" There was a frostiness in Susan's tone, like she was trying hard to sound normal and not remember the last conversation between them.

"Probably not; school work is really busy. Listen, I called to tell you that I've started seeing someone."

There was silence on the line. Elizabeth could almost feel her mother's fear, the question she both wanted to ask and didn't want to ask.

"Is he?" Susan said at last.

"Yes. He's disabled."

"No," Susan said. "No, I am not going to talk about this."

"Mom, this is my life. You can't close your eyes to it."

"What if this boy finds out about you and your . . . thing?"

"He knows," Elizabeth said, feeling a bit triumphant that she had already crossed that bridge.

"Oh, so you just go around telling people. That's great. I don't want the whole world knowing about you and sex."

"I'm not just talking to everyone! But sometimes it's relevant. I'm not going to pretend to be attracted to the same guys my friends are, it's dishonest and it hurts. But this is about Ethan. He's really nice, Mom. You'll like him. I want to bring him home."

"Absolutely not."

"Mom, come on, you're not being reasonable."

"I am not the one being unreasonable, Elizabeth. It's my choice and I am not going to discuss this anymore. You give me a call when you've come to your senses. When you've stopped with this foolishness."

"Fine," Elizabeth said and hung up the phone. She slid down her wall and lay on the bed staring at the other wall.

Chapter Thirteen

"Oh my God!" Elizabeth squealed when she opened her school email. There was no one around to hear the excitement. She jumped up and down a few times, then ran to her phone. She hesitated a moment, longing to type in her family phone and tell her mother the news. Then she remembered Susan tearing up her photographs and felt a wrench in her stomach. She dialed Ethan's number.

"They've picked my photographs!" she shouted into the phone.

"Who's what?"

"My photos are going on exhibit in the school gallery. I won the grant with the series that you modeled in."

"That's awesome," he said. "I knew you were going to get it."

"Thanks," Elizabeth said.

"Let's go and celebrate," Ethan suggested.

"I have to meet with Professor Higgins, but I'll come by after."

Elizabeth hung up and got ready. She finger-combed her hair and put on a new white t-shirt. In this moment, she felt like a real artist. The pride and excitement was everything she had hoped it would be.

When she walked into the professor's office she found it to be a cozy, small room with walls covered in dark-spined books.

"Hello, Elizabeth," Professor Higgins said, rising to greet her. She was a thick woman with dark skin and a mass of beautiful braids. "Congratulations."

"Thank you." Elizabeth smiled and she felt as though she were glowing. The professor indicated a chair and Elizabeth sat. She felt swallowed up by the large, stuffed chair.

"Your project," Professor Higgins said, "was ambitious and unique. Do you mind if I ask where your inspiration came from?"

Elizabeth's mouth dried up. What could she say? Why had she not prepared a good answer to this question?

"Um, I have a friend who is disabled," she said finally.

"Well, it's wonderful. Now, today what we're going to do is prepare the invitations and then we'll need to schedule a time to get the exhibit set up in the hall."

"Sounds great," Elizabeth said. Her chest relaxed as she realized that her excuse worked. Higgins wasn't going to ask her anything more about disability.

They spent the next couple of hours putting together a list of people to invite. Elizabeth was excited to see all the gallery scouts getting invited. She added her parents to the list too. She hadn't mentioned this to them at all, and knowing how her mother felt about her photographs, they probably wouldn't come. But she would make the gesture anyway.

Elizabeth went to Ethan's room after she and the professor finished with the invitations. When he opened the door she saw that he had filled his small room with wild flowers. There were vases of them every where she looked. Elizabeth laughed. "You've been busy," she said.

"Congratulations," he said and he kissed her. She wrapped her arms around his neck and ran her fingers through his hair. When they broke apart, he rested his forehead against hers. "Are you excited?" he said.

Elizabeth was surprised to find that this was a difficult question. There was much more than just excitement in her. The reality of it was sinking in. She was going to put these photographs about disability on display where anyone could look and see her interest. "Yes," she said, "but I'm nervous too."

They sat down together on his bed and he took her hand while she continued, "I feel like it exposes me too much. Now that I've won and I got that validation, I think maybe I should back out."

"No one is going to look at those pictures and think . . .you know," Ethan said.

"That I'm a pervert?" Elizabeth sat silently for a few moments. "I won. That's what I wanted. I proved mine were the best. Now I can withdraw."

"Why would you do that?"

"I'm not an in-your-face person. I'm shy, I'm background."

Ethan pulled her hand closer to him and she looked into his rich, warm eyes. "Are you sure about that?" he said.

"Yes! I've always been that way."

"I think you have an incredible opportunity here. And if you're going to make a career out of photography, you've got to be able to take risks."

"This is my life, Ethan. And you don't have any say." Elizabeth felt bad that she was getting defensive, but didn't think she could stop.

"I know, but I can offer some insight, I hope. You and others like you deserve to be heard, but I don't see anyone else in a position to own it the way you could. People need you. I mean, what does it mean for my future if people think that someone wanting to sleep with me should be a crime? They're wrong. I deserve to be with someone who loves my body. How am I going to convince people of that?"

Elizabeth bit her lip. "This is really difficult," she said.

Ethan ran his hand up and down her arm, her skin shivering under his touch. "I'll be right there with you," he said, "Every step of the way. You love this project, you put your heart and soul into it and I want it to be seen."

They looked at each other for a few minutes. Then Ethan said, "Do you want to order a pizza?"

Elizabeth still didn't move. As Ethan grabbed the headboard and pulled himself up, reaching for his crutches, she said, "You're right. We have to fight this. We have to be vocal. If I don't do it, who will?"

He grinned down at her. "That's the spirit."

"I'm ready to fight back against the prejudice. And I've got an idea." She sat up straighter and leaned forward, feeling energy coursing through her as the plan took shape in her mind. If she was going to expose herself, then she wouldn't go only half-way.

"It's good to see you excited about something," Ethan said.

"Listen, we're going to modify my project for the gallery display, but we only have a week and this is going to be huge. We have work to do." She told him the plan and he grinned.

"This is going to be awesome," he said, "but if you're afraid of people knowing the truth about you, this might not be the best way to go."

"I don't want to hide from it anymore. I want to just face it head on and go bold. If I'm afraid, then that's a reason to not hide."

"I admire your courage, Elizabeth. You live authentically and I really like that about you."

"Okay, I'm going to go reserve the studio again and I want you to contact the models, see who will be willing to help us."

"I'm on it. First thing tomorrow. Now, how about that pizza?"

The next morning, Elizabeth reserved the photo studio and the developing lab for as much time was available in the next week. She hoped Professor Higgins wouldn't be paying too much attention to which students were using the facilities. Although, Elizabeth could always claim that she was using it for another photography class.

After reserving the space, Elizabeth spent the afternoon with Higgins setting up the first exhibit in the gallery building on campus. She said nothing about her plans to change the entire thing before the big opening.

Ethan came through with the models and the two of them spent hours a day together in the studio redoing the entire semester-long project.

"You're going to pose for me again, right?" she said to Ethan, tracing her finger along the edge of his face.

He smiled. "Whatever you want," he said.

Late nights made them prone to laughing and also brought out more creativity in Elizabeth than she had ever felt before. With the lack of sleep she stretched the boundaries of what she could achieve with this project.

After all the new shots were taken, Elizabeth uploaded them onto the computer at the studio. She narrowed them down and Ethan sat on a rolling office chair behind her giving his input.

"Which of these do you think?" Elizabeth said, pointing to a series of five pictures of the same model.

"This one," Ethan said, pointing without hesitation.

"Thank God you're here," Elizabeth said. "I'd be stuck for years otherwise."

"Glad to help," he said, resting his arms on her shoulders and kissing her neck.

She giggled. "I don't know if that's helping."

"Sure it is. You need a break." He took her hands and guided her out of her chair, rolling back in his. "In fact," he said, "Now I'm the one with an idea." He let go of her hands and leaned down, got his hands to the floor and gently shifted his body onto the ground. Lying back on the floor, he looked up at her, and Elizabeth saved her work on the computer, then straddled his body on the ground. She pushed his crutches out of the way.

She leaned over him and kissed his cheek while he grazed her neck with his teeth. His warm breath on the thin skin of her neck sent shivers through her body. She sat back up and started peeling off her shirt and jeans. Ethan wiggled out of his pants and moved up against the wall, sitting up against it. Elizabeth climbed onto him and he wrapped his arms around her waist in a tight embrace. Elizabeth griped his shoulders, wanting to hold him so close that they melded into one. He moved her up and down as he pressed his cheek against her chest.

His curls tickled her chin each time she moved. The cold air of the studio contrasted against his warm arms and hands on her skin. She braced herself against the wall and planted her knees on either side of him. While she took over the speed, he gripped the sensitive, smooth skin of her butt. The sensations within her mingled and she gasped, suddenly grabbing his hair and pressing his face tight against her chest.

She fell back to the floor, rolling away from him and giggled. Ethan laughed. After a few minutes lying there, they began to put their clothes back on.

"Okay, help me up now," Ethan said. She stood and pulled him onto his unsteady feet. He leaned on the desk while she picked up his crutches and handed them to him.

"Well, let's go get some dinner," Elizabeth said. "Then we can come back and get everything printed out and mounted."

"All right, you first. I want to watch your butt while you walk."

"I want to watch yours!"

"My turn." He stuck out his tongue at her and she lightly socked him on the shoulder.

Suddenly serious, she said, "Thank you. I don't think I could have gotten through this experience without you."

"I love you," he said.

A grin spread across her face. "You do?"

"Yes." He nodded.

"I love you too." She kissed his cheek, then walked out ahead of him.

They went to a late-night diner and loaded up on comfort food and coffee. Back at the studio, Elizabeth began to print out the new photos and Ethan mounted them. Once they were all ready, Elizabeth loaded her arms with photographs and Ethan locked the studio behind them. It was still a few hours before dawn.

Elizabeth tried to stay out of the glow of the scattered campus street lights, but Ethan's unusual walk was far too noticeable if anyone happened to be looking. "How are we going to get in?" he hissed.

"I don't know," she whispered back. She was carrying all the prints in her arms, since Ethan needed his hands to walk. They were so large it was awkward to carry them.

"Wait, we got everything else ready and we don't even have a way in?"

"I can't think of everything."

They made their way around the outside of the building. The front door was locked, not surprisingly. Elizabeth could see a faint glow from the after-hour lights inside. On the far side she found what she was looking for, an unlocked window. "Bingo," she breathed.

"You want me to climb in a window?"

"Yes." She pushed it open and lowered the photos into the building, then slid in herself. She moved the pictures away from the window and came back to help Ethan. He passed his crutches in one at a time, then pulled his body over the ledge and tumbled inside, almost knocking Elizabeth over. He leaned on her shoulder while she handed his crutches back to him.

Together they pulled down all Elizabeth's previous work and hung up the new pictures. "My mother would faint if she saw this," he said as he hung one of himself.

Elizabeth grinned. "We're going to shock more than just your mother."

She stepped into the center of the room and surveyed their work. It was hard to fully get the effect with only the dim after-hour lights, but she was sure it was going to look spectacular tomorrow.

Chapter Fourteen

On the day of the show, Elizabeth went to Amy's house to get ready. Her friend did her hair and makeup as well as lending her a shimmery black dress. On Amy it was calf-length, but on Elizabeth it was knee-length.

Ethan showed up outside the house an hour before the show was scheduled to start. He called Elizabeth and she came out onto the porch and grinned when she saw that he was using his wheelchair.

"For the special occasion," he said, holding a hand up against the sun in his face.

Amy came out of the house behind Elizabeth. "Are you going to stay down there while we get ready?" she called down to Ethan.

"You're almost done, right?"

"Yes," Elizabeth said, poking Amy, "we're done."

"We're going to be early," Amy said.

"Oh, get my camera," Elizabeth said. She went down the stairs and sat on Ethan's lap. Amy snapped pictures of them. "You look hot," Elizabeth whispered in his ear.

"So do you," he said.

"Are you ready for the firestorm?"

"Definitely. This is going to be awesome."

Amy pulled her car out of the garage.

"Me and the chair will go in the back," Ethan said. He opened the back door and grabbed the top edge. He stood shakily and got one foot caught on the wheelchair, tripping forward into the car as he tried to disentangle it. "I know, I know," he said to the girls, "I'm too suave for my own good."

Elizabeth laughed, while Amy just looked relieved that he was able to poke fun at himself. Elizabeth pushed the empty chair to the other side and stowed it for him.

She got in the passenger seat and they drove towards campus.

As they parked, they could see people already pooling outside the exhibit hall. No one had seen it yet. Elizabeth's stomach tightened and she thought she might throw up. She was taking a huge risk and putting her biggest insecurity on display. On top of that she had all the expected fears of an artist showing her work for the first time. She had no idea what people were going to think.

As they approached the front, Ethan peeled off and went by himself up the ramp on the side. Elizabeth watched as he pushed up it, his shoulders rising and falling with each stroke. Then Elizabeth turned and saw her professor.

"Congratulations, Elizabeth," Professor Higgins said. "Are you ready?"

"I guess so," Elizabeth said. Her face flushed. What would the professor think when she saw the completely different exhibit about to be on display? Ethan reached them. "Professor, this is my boyfriend, Ethan."

"Oh, you're one of the models."

"That's right," Ethan said.

The doors were unlocked at that moment and they shuffled in with the other couple dozen people. The space looked fresh and virgin with the light pouring in from skylights. It was very different from the night before. There were a few gasps and people glancing at each other, but most remained composed, as though they saw pictures like this all the time. To be fair, they might.

A few clumps of fellow students, though, squinted their noses and raised eyebrows at one another. She heard a few muffled, "Oh my God's".

Elizabeth, Ethan, and Amy made their way to the middle of the room and Elizabeth surveyed the result. In oversize frames with light matting, all over the room, were black-and-white pictures of people with disabilities naked and provocatively posed.

Her favorite was a girl in a power wheelchair who had unusually shaped limbs. She had moved herself to drape across the chair sideways. Her limbs created interesting shapes against the backdrop and it was arrestingly beautiful. Ethan went back to his pretending-to-be-a-bad-boy pose leaning forward on his crutches with his shoulders turned in and looking fiercely at the camera, but this time completely naked.

Professor Higgins rushed over. "Elizabeth, what is going on?"

"I'm making a statement," she said.

"This is wonderful work, but the dean is going to be very upset."

"I hope this won't get you in trouble," Elizabeth said, suddenly realizing that this act had consequences outside of herself. "I'll be sure to tell him you had nothing to do with this."

The professor squeezed Elizabeth's shoulder. "Controversy and art go together. You've provoked people and that was the point of my class. Good job."

Ethan poked Elizabeth in the ribs and nodded his head towards the door. Elizabeth frowned. A man was wheeling up to the front door from the outside. Through the frosted glass she could only see an outline of his form. "Is that?"

"Yeah, it is," Ethan said.

The door slid open and Stewart glided in. He slowly wheeled towards her while looking at the pictures as he went. "Nice work," he said when he got to her. He grinned.

Elizabeth leaned down and threw her arms around his neck. "What are you doing here?" she said, tears of joy starting to sting in the corners of her eyes.

"Ethan invited me to see your show."

She turned to Ethan with shock on her face. "You did?"

"Yes. Just to see you look like that," he said, grinning.

"I love you guys," Elizabeth said. "Thank you for being here for me."

People kept coming up to Elizabeth, asking her questions and talking about photography. She soon lost track of Stewart and Ethan, but saw them again later in the foyer outside the exhibit. Stewart was showing Ethan how to do wheelies in his chair. Elizabeth smiled.

Professor Higgins brought over the gallery scouts. Elizabeth was relieved to find that she didn't have to say much. They spoke about the implications and artistic merit of the work without her having to add anything.

"We would like to move this exhibit into our space next month," one of them said.

Elizabeth felt faint. She reached for the wall. "Wow," she said, "That would be great." Professor Higgins gave her a proud smile.

Then the front door was opening again and Elizabeth's parents stood together in the entrance. Elizabeth watched as her mother's eyes became wide. Little splotches of pink appeared on her face. She stumbled and backed out of the room before she had even come all the way in.

Elizabeth was frozen to the spot for a moment. She had looked into her mother's face and seen something new. It was fear. Susan wasn't mean or angry; she was afraid of disabled people. How had Elizabeth not realized that before?

"Mom, wait." Elizabeth burst out the doors to the gallery and ran down the stairs. Her parents turned and looked at her. Suddenly she was at a loss.

"I'm sorry," she said. "I never wanted to hurt you."

Susan looked behind her and Elizabeth turned to see her ragtag little band of friends. Stewart and Ethan and Amy, watching, but too far back to hear.

When Elizabeth looked back to her parents, her dad had put his arm around her mother. In that moment Susan looked almost like a child. "Listen," she said to Elizabeth, but looking down, "I want you to bring Ethan to dinner next weekend."

Elizabeth nodded and smiled a small smile.

"Okay," Susan said and Elizabeth could see that it was as much as Susan could give at this moment. Her parents turned to leave again and Elizabeth watched. When they had driven away, she turned back to her friends, all watching at the top of the stairs.

She walked back to them and smiled. "We have an invitation for dinner," she said to Ethan, the relief making her shoulders sag.

"Good for you, man," Stewart said. "Elizabeth's parents are a tough crowd."

"Speaking of dinner," Amy said, throwing an arm over Elizabeth's shoulders, "When can we get out of here and celebrate at Lucca's?"

Elizabeth laughed. "Okay, let me check with the professor."

As she walked back into the gallery, it felt as though she were shedding some previous skin, leaving it lying on the ground in her wake, and her emerging self was as light as air.

BONUS STORY

A short story about what Stewart has been up to during this time.

***

"You just drove that dinky car of yours across the entire country?" Claire huffed into the phone. "Stewart, one of these days you are going to give me an ulcer."

"That's why I didn't tell you about it," he said, rolling down his car window and closing his eyes, smelling the salt air.. He was in California again, sitting in his car in the parking lot of his best friend's apartment building. His Aunt Claire continued to tell him how stupid he had been until Stewart finally interrupted her. "Claire, listen, I'm fine. I'm here. Everything is good. Can I talk to you later?"

"Oh, we will talk later. I have more to say to you. What if you had broken down in the middle of the country? What if you couldn't get help? Giving a little bit of latitude to your weaknesses is not a bad thing, it's a safe thing."

"I'm twenty-six years old, Aunt Claire, I can make my own choices."

"You just think about how your choices are going to affect everyone else if you die out on the road, unable to get help."

"Thinking about it right now, I'll get back to you." From here he could see his friend, Jeff's, apartment on the second floor. The window was open; he must be home.

"Oh Stewart," his aunt said with a sigh, "you know I only worry because I love you."

"I need to get a place to stay sorted out, okay? I'll talk to you later. I promise." He hung up his phone and pushed it into the front pocket of his jeans maneuvering against some resistance. He opened the car door, then leaned across to his passenger seat and grabbed the frame of his wheelchair, putting it on the pavement. Upended on the ground, the little caster wheels spun. He held it steady with one hand and attached the larger wheels one at a time with the other. They clicked easily into place. Getting a grip on the seat cushion, he shifted his butt onto the chair, then lifted his legs over one at a time. The whole maneuver took about thirty seconds. He slid his hands across the rails on his wheels, closed the car door, and locked it. He rested his hand on the door of the car for a moment, smiling at its faded blue. "Good girl," he said softly.

No one was in sight. It was a classic Los Angeles day with a comfortable heat and hardly a cloud in the sky. He pushed inside the building, glad that there was no reception area with a person to try to open the door for him and get in the way.

He entered the elevator and pressed the button for the second floor. During the brief ride up, he moved his cell phone from where it was threatening to burst back out of his pocket and stashed it in the pouch behind his legs. He rolled slowly down the hallway, pushing against the low carpet, and stopped at Jeff's door, giving a quick knock.

Jeff swung open the door and the look of surprise on his face was quickly replaced with a grin. "Back already," he remarked. "You just couldn't stay away."

That was the truth. "Good to see you too," Stewart said. Jeff moved back and Stewart rolled into the small apartment that he remembered so well.

"Do you want a beer?" Jeff said.

"Absolutely," Stewart said. He parked himself beside the sofa in the living room where he could see out the window to the balcony and the street that he had once run down in complete panic. Just looking at it, his heart began to beat a little faster. Jeff walked in and handed him a glass bottle beer, then slumped onto the sofa.

"Not that I'm complaining," Jeff said, "But I didn't see you for seven years and now I'm seeing you twice in six months. Didn't you have to get back to Massachusetts for the start of the school year?"

Stewart was in his last year of getting a teaching degree to become a high school science teacher. He looked away from the window and back to his friend. "I transferred," he said. "I was wondering if I could stay with you until I get set up here."

Jeff sat up straight suddenly. "Are you saying you're moving back?"

"That's what I'm saying."

Jeff clapped his hands and said, "This is going to be awesome."

Over the summer Stewart had reluctantly agreed to come back to California at Jeff's insistence. His friend had wanted him to give a speech at the annual surfing competition. There was a time when Stewart dominated that competition.

He had been surprised how nice it was to be back in the ocean, surfing again. When it came time to travel back to Massachusetts, he found himself reluctant to go. Stewart hadn't expected to feel torn as he left. The ocean was pulling him, drawing him to stay. California was his home. It was where he had been born. Despite all the running he had done, what he had left behind here would not stay quiet in his mind.

"You going to see your dad now that you'll be here longer than a few days?" Jeff said.

"Wasn't planning to," Stewart answered.

Jeff didn't pursue the subject. "You're totally welcome to stay here as long as you need."

"Great, my bag is in the car."

"Why don't we get it on the way back after the bar? I need to get down there. The kid I hired part time gets off in about twenty minutes."

"Sounds good."

"Cool, I'm going to call Lee and Leah and see if they want to meet up with us. It'll be just like old times."

Stewart chuckled to himself. Jeff's optimism was unbeatable. It was unlikely to be just like old times. The summer he was sixteen Stewart was the local surfing champion, Leah was his girlfriend, and Lee was always in his shadow.

Outside they started down the sidewalk towards the sunset.

"Are you okay to, you know, well...walk?" Jeff said.

Stewart looked up at his friend's concerned face and couldn't help the edge of his mouth twitching towards a smile. "I know where the damn bar is, Jeff. How many times have I crashed at your place?"

"Okay, yeah, but that was seven years ago. Things are different," Jeff said.

"Right," Stewart said, beginning to push down the street towards the bar. "I wasn't paralyzed."

"Now that you mention it," Jeff said, "I thought something was different."

Stewart laughed. "I'm not offended by the word 'walk,' okay? So don't worry about it."

Sand was brushed up over the sidewalk and it caught in Stewart's wheels, showering down over his hands. The warm air picked up salt from the ocean as it whipped down the beach. Jeff's small wooden shack rested right at the edge. People crowded around the doorway smoking, more leaned against motorcycles or strolled slowly down the boardwalk nearby. As they got closer, Stewart noticed the wooden ramp on the side of the stairs.

"This is new," he said, pushing himself up it.

"Someone told me I'd get a tax break," Jeff said, "But I think he lied."

"You need an incentive not to break the law?" Stewart called over his shoulder. Jeff followed him inside.

Stewart paused in the doorway to take in the scene. He had missed this place. Not much had changed in the years he'd been gone. There were a few tables, a long wooden bar, a small dance floor, everything in dark wood. This was where all the locals came. Jeff lived for this place, building it into the perfect hang out.

Leah was already there. She was leaning over the bar, wearing a mini skirt that didn't quite cover her butt and a sport's bra. Her warm honey skin glistened, still wet from swimming. The few patrons inside were all riveted to her. As Stewart's wheels rumbled onto the wooden floor, she turned and fixed him with her well-honed siren smile. Jeff gave her a wave, then went into the kitchen to get them food. Stewart slowly wheeled forward and Leah joined him at a table. He pulled a chair out of the way and slid into its place.

"No girlfriend this time, huh?" Leah said.

"Nope."

"Good. That kid was strange."

"Be nice, Leah. I care about Elizabeth a lot."

"Whatever." Leah leaned back and her eyes slowly looked him up and down. "Is your foot supposed to do that?"

"Huh?" Stewart looked down to see his foot shaking. "Oh yeah," he said. "Don't worry about that." He grabbed his knee and pulled the leg further in. "It'll stop in a minute."

"That's some weird shit," Leah said, throwing back her drink.

"I guess. Does it bother you?"

"Yeah, I'll be honest. It's hard to see you like this. I remember you in such a different way, you know?"

"You've changed too," Stewart said with a smile.

"Have not." Leah laughed, smacking his shoulder.

"Hey, I didn't hurt you, did I?"

"Are you kidding? These shoulders are as solid as granite," Stewart said, lifting the sleeve of his t-shirt.

Leah touched his neck and slid her hand down to his shoulders. "Oh my God, they are like one enormous brick wall." Her hand slid farther down his back to the top of the wheelchair.

"Hey, hey, "Stewart said, "Let's keep those hands where I can see them."

"Your foot stopped."

Stewart looked down. "Oh yeah."

"What does that mean? Like does that mean you could get better?"

"No."

"Sorry, I shouldn't have said."

"You can ask me whatever you want, Leah, we're friends. Really, whatever you want to know, just ask."

Leah smiled and put her bare foot against his crotch. "Does it still work?"

"Woah," Stewart said, rolling back. Her foot fell to the floor in front of her, an anklet jingling. She smiled at him.

"I really don't want to do this with you."

"Do what?" She leaned forward and smiled again, twirling a piece of her ocean-soaked hair in front of her.

Jeff came over with baskets of burgers and drinks and put them down. "So," Jeff said, "I was thinking that tomorrow we should catch the surf together, like old times."

"I can't," Stewart said, "I'm starting student teaching in the morning."

"Oh right," Jeff said.

"Saturday, though," Stewart said, "we can go Saturday morning."

Leah hadn't taken her eyes off Stewart and he was purposely not looking back at her. She wasn't really interested in him, this was all a game. A game she was good at and always had been. All she wanted to do was win, not actually follow through on any flirting. But Stewart liked to win too.

He decided to make her as uncomfortable as he possibly could. He pushed his hands against the seat of his wheelchair, shifting his body and thought *score one for me* when Leah looked away and fidgeted with her hair.

"If we get out early enough to beat the tourists," Jeff said.

"Yeah, maybe," Stewart said, looking at Leah. "But you know it takes me a while to get ready in the mornings these days."

She met his eye and he couldn't read her expression. She certainly didn't look disgusted or put off.

"What about Lee?" Stewart said. "It's not the old gang without your brother."

"He probably won't make it," Leah said.

"He hasn't been able to look at me since I came back in a wheelchair," Stewart said, slapping his lap for emphasis.

"Oh, so he's an ass," Leah said, "What else is new?"

Stewart started laughing. He couldn't keep up the pretense. "Tell him I want to talk to him."

"He's scared to death of you."

"I know. And it's ridiculous."

Jeff went back to the bar to serve more customers.

"Are you staying at a hotel?" Leah asked.

Stewart shook his head. "I'll crash on Jeff's couch until I find a place."

"Isn't a hotel easier for you? With, you know, the wheelchair and all?"

"No. Most hotels are not nearly as accessible as they think they are. A lot easier to get Jeff to help me out than try to deal with them."

While they ate, Leah's eyes wandered around the place. Stewart guessed she was looking for a new victim to charm.

"I'm going to head back to Jeff's, I have to get up early tomorrow for teaching."

Leah smiled. "You're getting old. And yet, somehow I stay the same."

"Ha. Ha," Stewart said flatly. He rolled over to the bar and got Jeff's keys.

***

Stewart opened his eyes to a still dark room, but Jeff was standing over him. Stewart started back against the pillow on the couch arm. "What are you doing?" he croaked, his voice still asleep.

"Are you okay?" Jeff said.

Stewart rubbed his eyes with one hand. "I was making noise?"

"Yes, a lot of noise."

"Sorry. Bad dreams."

"Dude."

"I know, I know."

Jeff stumbled back towards his room and Stewart sighed. He had been prone to nightmares for years, always happening when he was stressed. Maybe he was more nervous about the student teaching than he had thought.

In the morning he put on the new khaki pants and button down shirt that he'd bought just for this. When he left the apartment, Jeff wasn't awake. He stopped at a drive through for a coffee, then headed for the school.

When he entered the building, a petite woman with curly brown hair and thick-rimmed glasses came out of an office and walked towards him.

"You must be Stewart," she said, holding out her

hand.

Stewart shook it and said, "That's me." No doubt his professor had told her to be on the look out for a man in a wheelchair. Nice and easy to identify him.

"I'm Betsy," she said. "I'm told that you've already done some observation in the classroom." She started to walk down the hall. Stewart kept pace with her, the wheeling smooth and easy on the waxed tile floor. "Do you feel comfortable getting right into the teaching?"

"Sure," he said.

At the door to the classroom, Betsy held it open and waited for him to roll through. Fifteen pairs of eyes fixed on him as soon as he entered. He grinned, but kept his gaze on where he was going, the front of the classroom. There was a tall, thick slab of a desk typical of science classrooms. He pulled up in front of it and looked at the children while Betsy introduced him. "This is Mr. Masterson," she said. "He'll be doing lessons for the rest of the quarter."

These kids were eleven and twelve. Their eyes were curious, but they were waiting to see what he was like before anyone said anything. Stewart twisted in his chair and pulled a folder out of his backpack. There was no where to put the folder down, though, since the teacher desk was higher than his head. He rested it on his lap.

"I understand that this week you've been talking about the laws of motion. Who wants to fill me in?"

The girl front and center was happy to show off her knowledge. There was one in every classroom. When the girl was finished, Stewart took out some transparencies with cartoons illustrating motion. He pulled around the large desk to get to the screen above the blackboard. When he reached for the cord he found that its end was several inches above his hand.

He could feel all the eyes in the room on the back

of his head. There was no way he was going to be able to reach the cord. Things like this made it look like he was less competent than an able-bodied teacher, even though it was the environment that was the problem, not him. Would the observing teacher report that he wasn't fit for the job because of this? Could he ask her to tie an extra string to it for him? He swallowed, then turned around with a smile on his face. "Who wants to help me get the screen in place?"

Betsy rushed forward to do it while the kids just stared. Next time Stewart would have to find a way to involve the kids in helping him. It would connect them to him and make them feel more confident. There was still some awkwardness after the slides.

"Okay," Stewart said, "Look at me." He turned so he was sideways to the kids and lifted his hands off his wheels. "If I want to move forward, what would I do? Pull or push?"

That got their attention. Stop trying to ignore his wheelchair and use it instead. He showed them forward, backward, turning, and wheelies. Before the bell rang, Stewart said, "You've done great, so I'll open up for some not physics related questions."

"What's wrong with your legs?" The boy who asked got smacked in the arm by the girl sitting beside him.

"That's all right," Stewart said, "I'm not surprised it's on your mind. Have you guys taken biology yet?"

The kids nodded.

"Well, I was in an accident where my spine was broken. The nerves were torn and I was paralyzed. When you break a bone in your leg or your arm, it can heal. The spine doesn't do that. So my legs are affected only because they aren't getting information from my brain anymore."

This opened a floodgate of questions and Stewart

answered each one until the bell rang. After the kids had run out, Betsy said, "I think that went very well. I'll see you tomorrow." Stewart breathed a sigh of relief. With the first day down, it was only going to get easier.

Even though Stewart told Jeff he had no intention of visiting his father, after school each weekday he found himself in the neighborhood. He took to parking across the street and just looking at the house. He hadn't been inside since he was fourteen years old and his father had sent him to the east coast to live with his aunt. Considering how badly his father wanted to erase the past, Stewart was surprised he still living in the house where Stewart's mother had died.

But he knew they were there. He saw the family coming and going. A perfect little unit without him. From afar he observed his two little step sisters who had grown so tall and beautiful that he would not have recognized them if he hadn't seen them with his father.

Stewart didn't know why he kept watching them. He didn't know what he expected to do, but he didn't plan to ever talk to them. When he got back to Jeff's each late afternoon, his friend never asked where he had been.

One Wednesday Stewart watched as Ellen returned to the house alone. He suspected she had dropped the girls off for some activity. She parked her car and got out.

Ellen was utterly different from how he remembered her. She was smaller and more meek. Without his cloud of anger he could see the twitchy worry on her face, the way she never looked sure of herself. How could he have screamed at this poor woman? Regret circled his chest. The only thing he had noticed about her back then was that she was so very different from his mother.

Then Stewart realized she was looking back at him. She frowned and began to walk towards his car.

Stewart fumbled with his key, hurrying to get away before she realized who he was. She was beside the car before he could pull away, though.

She stood just to the side of the driver's door and frowned, looking in at him. He could practically see the gears turning in her head as she tried to work out why he looked familiar. Then her hand flew in front her mouth and her eyes filled with tears. She walked closer and he rolled down the window.

"Stewart?" she whispered.

"Hey, Ellen," he said.

There was fear in the creases around her eyes. She was thinking about the same moment he was, he was sure of it. In the stairwell of the house behind her, late at night, the only light from the open door of a bathroom on the second floor, her thin body pressed against the wall, and his hands holding her there.

"It's been so long," she said. She seemed to be having trouble figuring out what else to say. Though Stewart had seen his father most Christmases, he hadn't seen Ellen in twelve years. After that night when Ellen had confronted him for coming home wasted and he had left marks on her skin from shoving her against the wall, his father had shipped him off to South Carolina to live with Aunt Claire. He hadn't seen his step-mother since.

"You should come in," she continued.

"It's not that simple," Stewart said, glancing behind her to the series of steps up to the front door of the house.

"It is. Really, Stewart. The past is the past. I've so wanted the chance to talk to you again."

"No, I mean I really can't."

"What do you mean? We haven't seen you, I mean I haven't seen you in years, and here you are. Don't you want to talk?"

"I can't come in because of the stairs on the

house."

She tilted her head and frowned. He realized that she couldn't see the logo on his license plate and her gaze hadn't shifted from him long enough to take in the jumble of wheels and tubes on the seat beside him. She had no idea that he was paralyzed. "Wait a minute," he said. "My dad never told you?"

"Told me what?"

"Well, isn't that just like him?"

"I don't understand."

Ellen moved back as Stewart opened the car door and shoved his thin legs out onto the ground. The surprise movement caused one of them to start shaking. "I can't walk," he said.

Ellen opened her mouth then closed it again. She looked for a long time just at his legs. He followed her gaze down his jeans that looked like they would fit a twelve year old to his feet in sneakers on their sides, not flat against the ground as they would be if he were going to stand. He just let her look, gave her time to process it.

Slowly Ellen's eyes rose back to his face and Stewart could read every emotion behind her eyes: shock, relief, then pity. Her tense body relaxed at last. "How long?" she said.

"Seven years," Stewart said.

"Richard never said."

She was so easy to read. He saw her trying to reconcile that her husband had never mentioned her step-son almost dying and being paralyzed. "He wishes I didn't exist," Stewart said, "It's okay."

"I never wanted that, Stewart. I hope you know that. I wanted us to be a family."

"It's not your fault. It's something between me and Dad."

"Can I tell him you were here?"

"If you must," Stewart said. "I wouldn't

recommend it, though."

"Are you living in the area now?"

"Yeah, I just moved back."

"I'd like to be able to reach you. Maybe we could start fresh."

Stewart nodded. "That's fair. Let me give you my phone number."

Ellen took it, then reached forward and gave his shoulder a gentle squeeze. "Good to see you," she said. He watched as she walked to the house, then he pulled his legs back in and drove to Jeff's.

The apartment was empty when he got back, so he did some school work and ate chips from the cabinet. When it started getting late he took off towards the bar. As he got close he saw Leah sitting on a curb outside. Her eyes were gazing in an unfocused way at the pavement in front of her. No one else was around. Stewart changed course and headed for her. He pulled up in front of her. Leah looked at his feet and slowly, unsteadily, her gaze rose up the rest of his body to his face.

"Hey, Stewart!" She smiled.

"How drunk are you?" he said.

She flicked her hand dismissively. He leaned forward and gripped her elbow while holding onto his wheelchair with his other hand to keep his balance.

"Let me get you home," he said. She stood, then leaned over him, her long dark hair brushing against the sides of his face.

"I knew you couldn't resist me," she whispered and her breath was warm against his forehead, smelling of beer and raspberries. He closed his eyes and clutched the seat of his chair for a moment to get control over himself. *It isn't real*, he reminded himself.

"Where do you live?" he said.

"This way." She started to walk forward, but she was unstable and her long legs seemed to be everywhere at once. Stewart was afraid he was going to run over her feet.

His phone began to ring. He frowned and grabbed it out of the pouch behind his legs. Pete's mother's name appeared on the screen. Stewart felt the guilt tightening in his chest. "Hang on," he said to Leah, "I need to take this." Leah nodded and promptly sat down on Stewart's lap. He tried to disentangle himself from her limbs as he answered, but she wrapped her lanky arms around his neck and rested her head on his shoulder.

"Ms. Morris," he said into the phone. "How are you?"

"I hate this time of year," she said.

"I do too," he said. It was the gray period in between when Pete died in the summer and his birthday near Christmas. Stewart had never told Ms. Morris that Pete's death was partly his fault. All she knew was that he had tried to save her son and had sacrificed the use of his legs to do it.

"Do you ever feel like you're in the wrong life and your real life is waiting for you to get back to it?"

"Yes," Stewart said. He knew exactly what she meant. Each morning while he did his stretches he had a moment while touching the legs that he couldn't feel where he disbelieved that this was his body.

Leah began to kiss his neck and he swatted at her with one hand.

"The house is so empty," Ms. Morris said.

"Have you thought about moving to another place?"

"I don't think I can."

"That's okay."

"I want to visit you."

"I'd like that," Stewart said. He said goodbye and hung up the phone.

"Who was that?" Leah said.

"It was Pete's mother." Stewart pushed forward and Leah gripped him tighter to keep from falling off his lap. She frowned. "Why is she calling you? That was seven freakin years ago and you did what you could. I mean, look at you."

Stewart's jaw tightened as it did every time someone told him that he had done his best to save Pete. He swallowed hard and tried to keep his voice light. "She needs someone to listen to her."

"Whatever," Leah said and she returned to nibbling at his neck. The warmth of her breath sent shivers through his torso.

"Are there stairs at your place?" Stewart said, both to change the topic and because he wanted to know if he'd be able to see her in.

She grinned at him.

"Leah, focus. Are there stairs at your place?"

"I'm on the first floor," she said in a low voice, running her fingers through his hair and giving a mild tug.

"Pay attention so you can direct me," he said.

"Turn right up there." She pointed towards several tall palm trees, outlined against an inky blue sky.

When they got to her door, Leah tried to fit her key in the lock, but kept missing. Stewart reached around her and touched her hand. The skin was as smooth as he remembered, buffed by the sand. He closed his hand over hers and directed the key into the lock.

The apartment was a single room, strewn with clothes. Stewart forced his wheels over the obstacles on the floor with some annoyance. He didn't care at this point if he left tire tracks on her clothes. He hoisted her off his lap and she landed on the mattress on the floor. She giggled, rolling onto her back and fixing him with her sparkling dark eyes.

"All the men around here are such jerks," she

said.

"Right. So you come to me." Stewart sighed, but she was already passed out, her head back and her arms wide. *If all the men are jerks, who do you turn to? The one guy you don't see as a real man.*

Stewart left, making sure the door was locked behind him.

***

Stewart woke to the sound of his cell phone ringing. Bleary eyed, he felt around beside the couch until he found his empty wheelchair and grabbed the phone out of the pouch.

"Hello?" he said.

"Stewart, this is Ellen," his step-mother said. Her voice sounded tight.

"What's wrong?" he asked.

"It's your father. He's had a stroke."

"Oh my God."

"And I just don't know what to do. He's going to be okay, they say, but it'll be a long recovery. They'll send him home in a few days and I can't deal with him all by myself."

"I'm sorry," Stewart said.

"You've got to come. He doesn't listen to me, but I know you can get through to him."

"I can't even get into the house, how am I going to help?"

"I'll have a ramp put in. Please, Stewart. He needs you."

"He doesn't need me, he hates me. He's been trying to pretend I don't exist for the past twenty years." Stewart pinched the bridge of his nose. "He's going to be furious when he finds out you invited me."

"Does that mean you'll come?"

Stewart sighed. "Yeah, it does."

Stewart hung up and put the phone back, then

rubbed his eyes and groaned. It was too late to go back to sleep. He had to get up for teaching.

In the afternoon Stewart began to gather his things back into his duffel bag. He'd just gotten his toothbrush from the bathroom when Leah burst through the door.

"Beat it, Jeff," she said.

"Hey!" Jeff responded from the kitchen, "This is my apartment."

Leah turned and fixed him with a stare, raising one eyebrow and he slunk into the hallway.

"What happened to you last night?" Leah demanded, turning on Stewart. One hand was on her hip.

"You passed out," Stewart said, "I went home."

"I don't get you, Stewart." She walked over to the couch where he had been spending his nights and sat down with her legs wide.

"What's not to get?"

"Stop packing for a minute and talk to me. You weren't even going to tell me you were moving?"

"I'm just going to my dad's." He put his duffel bag on the floor and stopped moving, facing her.

"Why do you keep putting me off?"

"Come on, Leah, I know you don't really want washed up old me."

"You must have a pretty low opinion of me if you think that I can't deal with you being in a wheelchair."

"Be honest with me and be honest with yourself."

"You act like you're totally comfortable and secure with your disability, but maybe you're the one who needs to be honest with themselves. I swear to God, when I look at you I just see Stewart. The same Stewart I loved as a kid. The changes are just details."

"I wish I could believe that, but I know the kind of men you date and it's not me."

"Sure," Leah said, snorting. "You know

everything. Clearly my pattern is jerks." And she left the apartment, pulling the door shut behind her with as much force as her lean, muscular arms could manage. The entire apartment seemed to shake.

The door opened slowly and Jeff gingerly walked back in. "What the hell did you say to her?"

Stewart glared at him. "I don't want to talk about it." He continued to pack his things into his duffel bag.

"You're about to explode," Jeff said.

"I'm fine."

"Look, I understand, it's more than you expected. After hiding away from all us lunatics, it's got to be difficult to come back and deal with us again."

"You're cool," Stewart said, a smile creeping onto his face, "I got no problem with you. The others I can handle. I've had plenty of people in South Carolina and Massachusetts wanting things from me too. I have it under control."

"You sure about that?"

"Yeah," Stewart said, not at all convinced himself.

He threw his bag into the back of his car and pulled his body into the driver's seat. While he disassembled his chair and put it on the seat beside him, he wondered what he would find at his father's house. He had to admit he was curious to see the inside of the house again, to see how it had changed and whether it still felt the same or not. He called Ellen and let her know he was on his way.

She had done as she said and there was an aluminum ramp over the stairs. It was steep and it creaked and shook as Stewart wheeled up, but it worked. When the door opened Stewart saw the two girls standing in front of him. They just stared at first.

"Hey," he said. "Remember me?"

They were eerily similar, both tall and thin with long blonde hair, both wearing tight jeans and layers of different colored t-shirts. Both nodded at him. One was slightly taller than the other. Stewart tried addressing her. "You're Samantha, right?" he said.

"Yes," the shorter one said. "And I'm Sylvia."

"You were this tall when I left," Stewart said, holding his hand out flat at the same level as the top of his wheel.

"Mom said you were coming back," Samantha said, her voice much softer than her younger sister.

"And you didn't believe her, did you?" Stewart said.

"I did at first," Sylvia said. "But you didn't and you didn't and you didn't."

Stewart nodded. "I'm sorry about that," he said. They were all quiet for a moment, then Stewart said, "So, has Dad been behaving himself?"

The girls giggled.

"I'll take that as a no. Lead the way."

They stepped back and Stewart pulled up on his wheels to get over the edge of the doorway. He followed the two girls down the hall. He wheeled slowly while he looked around. A lot was different: new paint color on the wall, new pictures hanging, new types of decorations. He wouldn't have known it was the same house.

"He's in there," Sylvia whispered, indicating the back den. The girls backed away. They didn't seem to want to go anywhere near their father. Stewart rolled to the doorway and gently nudged the door open with his knees.

Inside, the room was dim. A single tall lamp in the corner cast an orange glow across a circle of the floor. The room was set up as a study, but there was now a twin bed with white sheets blocking the rust colored couch. It didn't look like it belonged. Beside the bed was a large, boxy wheelchair with stickers on it indicating the hospital it came from.

His father was laying on his side on the bed. Richard's face hadn't been shaved in several days and his clothes were stained. He looked like a vagrant Ellen had found on the side of the road more than he looked like Stewart's father. The face of the man didn't move much, but his eyes were staring at Stewart with rage and hatred. To the side, Ellen was kneeling on the ground and trying to change Richard's socks.

She stopped as Stewart came in and the look on her face was gratitude and relief.

"What are you doing here?" Richard said and Stewart was startled by the way the words ran together even though he knew that his father's speech could easily have been affected by the stroke.

"I'm an expert on 'can't move'," Stewart said. He rolled farther into the room.

Richard grunted and moved his eyes down to the carpet. Ellen stood and lightly ran over to Stewart. "Thank you so much for coming," she said. "Can I talk to you out in the hall?"

Stewart nodded and backed up out of the room. Ellen closed the door gently behind her.

"He needs help with everything and he yells about it," she whispered. "I'm so frazzled."

"It's okay," Stewart said. "I can handle him." He knew that Ellen wasn't used to seeing the angry side of Richard. He reserved that for the people he didn't respect. "So what's his situation?" Stewart asked.

"He's needing to relearn a lot of motion and he is weak on his left side. We have a physical therapist coming to the house each day, but a lot of the time it's just me and I have to go to work. Will you be able to stay with him?"

Stewart nodded. "Student teaching ends next week and then I'll be free."

Ellen looked down at the floor and said even

more softly, "You still have money from your mother?"

Stewart swallowed. "Yeah," he said, "I do."

"We'll pay for your food and you living here and all that, of course."

"Sure. It's no problem. Go on now," Stewart said, nodding to the rest of the house. "Let me take care of it."

Ellen smiled and leaned down to take his hands from his lap and squeeze them. "Bless you," she said.

Stewart went into the room again, this time alone. Richard's eyes were closed and he didn't respond when Stewart came back in. Stewart assessed the room and decided he needed to get the rug out of the way. It was a thick, patterned rug and Stewart could tell just by looking at it that he wouldn't be able to wheel over it. While his father lay quietly, Stewart leaned over and rolled the rug, pushing it with his feet until it was against the far wall.

"What are you doing here?" Richard groaned from the bed.

Stewart looked at him. "Helping," he said.

"I don't need you."

"Sure," Stewart said, "why don't we get you up so I can change those sheets?"

Richard snorted and didn't move. Stewart grabbed hold of the ugly, shiny wheelchair that was so different from his own. He pulled it to the side of the bed and set the brake. Then he pulled himself as close to the bed as he could get and set his own brake.

Stewart leaned over, one hand on the edge of his chair to keep his balance, the other getting under his father's good arm. "Okay, here we go." Thank goodness for the core muscles he still had. "Are you going to help or what?"

"What's the point?" Richard said.

Stewart ignored him and dragged his father into the chair without help. He gave it a solid push to get it out of the way and went to find the sheets. Richard slumped and watched as Stewart fixed up the bed.

"Do you need to use the bathroom?" Stewart asked.

Richard glared at him.

"Right," Stewart muttered. He turned his father towards the bathroom, then got behind him and nestled his knees against the canvas back of the other chair. His arms burned with the effort of pushing both of them, but it worked. In the bathroom there was a seat over the toilet and Stewart helped his father onto it. Then he backed out of the room to give him privacy.

When Stewart came back in Richard said, "Is this what you do? With this stupid thing?" He rolled his head at the raised toilet seat with handles.

"No," Stewart said while getting Richard back in the other wheelchair.

Richard made a skeptical sound. Stewart said, "You don't need to worry about how I use the bathroom, okay?"

Before getting his father back into bed, Stewart finished changing the socks that Ellen had been trying to do. He bent down and when he was finished, he pushed his body back up by gripping his own knees and pushing up with his arms.

He got Richard back into bed and covered him with a blanket, then left him alone.

***

Stewart finished his student teaching and then he stayed at the house, prodding Richard and taking care of him while being treated with sullen silence or insults. He wondered how long he would keep doing this. His father was definitely making improvement and the physical therapist frequently reassured Ellen that a full recovery was likely.

Stewart suspected that Ellen was hoping this situation might connect him to his father again. Stewart doubted that was going to happen. Richard still hated him and it wasn't as though helping him to get dressed or use the bathroom was making them bond as father and son.

One day while Stewart was doing some exercises on Richard that the physical therapist had shown them, his cell phone rang. Stewart put down his father's leg and said, "I'll be right back."

He backed to the edge of the room and looked at the phone. It was his aunt's number.

"Claire?" he said.

"Actually it's John," his uncle said.

"Is everything okay?" Stewart glanced back at Richard, who was trying to turn over and kicking all the sheets off the bed in the process.

"Not exactly," John said.

Suddenly he had all of Stewart's attention and nothing in the room registered anymore. "Oh my God. Are Claire and the kids…?"

"They're fine. It's Ms. Morris."

Though the room returned to normal, Stewart felt his chest tightening. "What's happened?" he said.

"I'm sorry, Stewart, but she's taken her life."

Stewart could think of nothing to say. He felt the world change in that instant as his mind tried to re imagine it without Pete's mother. All the years since Pete died Stewart had kept in touch with her, tried to keep her going. It was the only way he could see to redeem himself from his role on that stormy July day.

"Stewart?" John said. "Are you okay?"

"Yeah," he said. He took a deep breath. "Listen, I'm not going to be able to go to the funeral, they need me here."

"I don't need a babysitter," his father piped up from the other side of the room.

"Shut up," Stewart called over his shoulder.

"It's okay," John said over the phone. "Everyone

knows how much you helped her over these last few years."

"Thanks for telling me." Stewart hung up and sat still for several minutes, the phone still in his hand.

"My sister okay?" Richard said and Stewart's attention snapped back.

"Yes." Stewart turned and wheeled back to the bed. "It's Ms. Morris. She killed herself."

Richard snorted. "Is that all? That crazy bitty finally offed herself. About time she put herself out of her misery."

Stewart's anger coursed through him so quickly that before he realized what he was doing he had grabbed hold of his father's arm and was squeezing tight.

Richard smiled. "You see?" he said, "I know the real you. And you're no different. You're just as violent as ever, nothing has changed."

Stewart let go and stared into his father's face. Was it true? Had he not changed from the angry little boy he had been? He swallowed hard. His phone, resting on his lap, beeped and Stewart looked down at a text message from Jeff. *Come by the bar tonight?* Stewart picked it up and texted back, *Absolutely. On my way.*

"I'm going to go," he whispered. He pivoted and pushed out of the room with Richard laughing behind him. "That's right," Richard said, "Run away."

Stewart found his step-mother and told her that he needed a break.

"Of course," Ellen said. She squeezed his shoulder. "Everything okay?"

"Yeah. Just someone I know died."

"Oh, I'm so sorry, Stewart."

Stewart nodded. "I'm going to go out for a while."

"Sure," Ellen said.

When he got to the bar, it was busy. Jeff was

running back and forth from the kitchen and barely had time to even nod. As Stewart looked around the room his gaze stopped when he saw Lee, who had not yet noticed him in the crowd. Suddenly this was looking like a set up. He knew Jeff well enough to recognize it. His friend must have seen Lee there and told Stewart to come without mentioning it to Lee. And Jeff was right. Stewart did want to talk to Lee.

He edged his way through the people, muttering, "Excuse me" every few moments and trying not to run over toes. When Lee looked up and caught sight of Stewart, his eyes grew large and he glanced around as though looking for a door to escape through.

Stewart rolled directly in front of him and said, "What is your problem?"

Lee looked down, watching his shoe as it scuffed at a mark on the floor. "I don't have a problem," he said.

"Look at me," Stewart said. He waited until Lee finally raised his eyes from the ground. "We need to talk about what happened to Pete and what happened to me, let's go outside where we can get some privacy." The look in Lee's eyes was fear. Stewart wondered what his old friend thought he could do to him.

Behind the bar, on a strip of boardwalk between it and the beach, next to a dumpster, they found a private space.

"You froze," Stewart said. "You didn't do anything."

Lee swallowed, then nodded. "How did you know?"

"Jeff told me."

Lee looked away, crossed his arms.

"Look," Stewart said, "It's okay. It happens. None of us knew what to do." He paused, then took a guess at what was bothering Lee. "I'm not upset that you have your career."

"Yeah, right," Lee muttered.

Stewart shook his head and smiled. "I hope you'll believe me. I think things happened how they happened and there's no point trying to figure out what we could have done differently. If we did that, I wouldn't have teased Pete and he wouldn't have been out in the ocean in the first place."

Lee nodded.

"You're suffering too," Stewart said, "I know you are. It's got to be hard that no one can see your wounds, while mine are obvious."

"I can't stop thinking about it," Lee said. "Over and over in my mind. I mean, shit man, look at yourself."

"I'm fine, Lee, trust me."

"How did Jeff manage to get his wits together and call 911?"

Stewart shrugged. "Luck?"

That night, long after everyone had gone to bed, Stewart returned to his father's house. The door creaked open and he rolled into the dark hallway. He thought about packing his bag and leaving right now. Richard wasn't interested in mending anything between them and it wasn't Stewart's job to change that. Things could go back to the way they had been.

Some part of him already knew he wasn't going to give up. He would see this project through, make sure his father was healed and then he would find his own place and see his sisters there once in a while. That would be it.

In the morning Stewart continued his routine as though Richard had never upset him.

"Came slinking back, did you?" Richard said when Stewart brought in his breakfast.

"Just eat," Stewart said. Richard was able to feed himself now, a noticeable improvement from when Stewart first arrived. When Richard had finished, Stewart moved into place to help him get into the other wheelchair and into the bathroom. With his arm over Stewart's shoulder, Richard muttered, "Life like this isn't worth it."

Stewart rolled his eyes. "You know what? It isn't all or nothing. I've been living for years with less than full function and it's completely doable. You don't have to give up as soon as you lose a little bit. Grow up."

"That's rich."

"Can we just get through this? Talking isn't necessary."

"You don't know," Richard said, his hot breath hitting Stewart's face. "You don't know anything."

"Fine."

"I didn't deserve this," Richard muttered. Stewart stopped in the doorway to the bathroom and looked at his father. "And I did?" he said.

Richard didn't answer, but the look on his face said that's exactly what he thought. "You think that I deserved to get paralyzed?" Stewart continued.

Richard looked at him, eyes burning with anger. "You were such a brat. Stubborn, difficult,diffident."

"I lost my mother," Stewart said.

"And I lost my wife. You didn't care how I felt."

"I was six!"

A voice behind them said, "Is this a bad time?"

Stewart twisted his chair and saw Leah standing in the doorway. He frowned. "What are you doing here?" he asked.

"You might not stand up for yourself, but I'm your friend and I will." She walked closer to where Richard was in the bathroom and Stewart just outside it. Looking right at his father, she said, "Your son is a good man. You're lucky to have him. I hope you can see that. Don't be such an ass to him."

Both men were too surprised to say anything and Leah turned and strode out of the room.

"Who was that?" Richard said.

"We used to date," Stewart said.

"What a looker," Richard said. "Not surprised you couldn't hang on to her."

"Yeah," Stewart said.

Once he got his father back into bed Stewart felt his own exhaustion. Jeff was right, he was close to bursting. Definitely time for him to visit his favorite place and get some peace. He slipped by the kitchen where Ellen and the girls were eating without them seeing him and got out the front door. While he drove towards the beach, he wondered about Leah showing up like that. Had Jeff told her to? Did she really think telling Richard off was going to help? He had to admit it felt nice that she had made the attempt.

There was one spot that he always went to relax and reflect. No one else came to this corner, far from the tourist attractions. He sat at the edge of the boardwalk and watched small waves getting tangled in rocks. Between the rocks and him there was sand that was almost as white as snow. The air was thick with salt and all was silent except for the rushing sound of the water itself.

Behind him he heard light footsteps against the wooden boardwalk. When he turned his head, Leah was walking towards him, barefoot with flip-flops tangling from one hand.

"I swear to God," Stewart said, "How do you people get by without me?"

Leah sat down beside him, her butt on the sandy wood of the boardwalk. He could only see the top of her head. "We manage," she said. "You don't have to take it all on by yourself, you know."

They sat side by side in silence for a few minutes. Then Stewart said, "Pete's mother is dead."

"I'm sorry," Leah said. They both continued to

look down towards the water. "Why does it bother you so much?"

Stewart crossed his arms. "I wanted to help," he said. "The truth is, if not for me, Pete never would have been trying to surf during that storm. I goaded him into it."

"Wow," Leah said.

"Yeah. I thought if I could help his mother, I could fix what I'd done."

Leah scooted closer to his chair and leaned her head against the side of his knee. "You brought her peace. I'm sure of it. And it's time for you to let it go."

"Do you think I've changed?" Stewart said. "Have I become a better person than the one who taunted Pete?"

"Take it from me," Leah said, "I've known you most of your life and you have changed. You're not that cocky boy anymore. Don't keep beating yourself up over the past. We were all dumb kids."

Leah stood up and walked down onto the sand, turning back with the wind blowing her hair in all directions. Stewart couldn't help thinking she looked like a sea goddess. "Come join me," she said.

"Do you think that's a good idea?" he asked.

"I think it's the best idea I've ever had."

He smiled. He leaned over his legs and placed one hand flat on the sand, but it was too soft and he ended up tumbling out of his wheelchair onto the beach, laughing. His legs were twisted around each other.

Leah giggled and grabbed his ankles, pulling him down towards her and straightening his body in the process. Though it was dark out, the air was still warm. Leah climbed up Stewart, straddling him. He looked up at her dark eyes and wondered at how strange it was that when they were teenagers, he had never taken a moment to really just look at her. Then she leaned forward and pressed her lips on his. He reached his arms around her and held her tightly against himself. He smelled deeply of her salty hair and honey skin.

"We're good together," Leah said, "And you know it."

"Yes," Stewart said, surrendering. "We are."

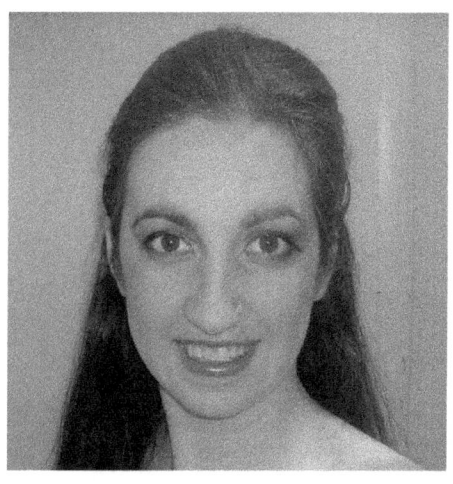

There isn't enough fiction out there with characters who have disabilities. Ruth Madison aims to fix that.

After years of combing through the dusty back shelves of libraries looking for her elusive, imperfect hero, she started writing her own.

Ruth's romantic tales are full of wounded heroes: men physically challenged by life, but not defeated. These men overcome the difficulties of amputation, paralysis, or cerebral palsy to find acceptance, happiness, and heroines who love them exactly as they are.

Visit Ruth at her website: RuthMadison.com or find out about new and upcoming releases at DevLovePress.com

Reviews are greatly appreciated! Take a minute and stop by your favorite web book seller and let people know what you thought!

COMING DECEMBER 2012 FROM DEV LOVE
PRESS...

THE BOY NEXT DOOR
BY ANNABELLE COSTA

I wasn't too happy when my parents told me that I had to try to make friends with the crippled kid who just moved in next door.

I was eight years old. For my entire life thus far, our next door neighbor in a suburb of Pittsburgh, was an ornery old woman named Agnes. Why are all old people named Agnes, for some reason? Not that I'm prejudiced against old people or anything. My grandmother, Nana, lived with us and was never an ornery bitch, and probably still the best cook I've ever known. Anyway, Agnes failed to wake up one morning, and the house got sold off to a young family with two kids.

I was initially really psyched to find out that the family had two kids, one of whom was allegedly my age. I pictured a girl with blond pigtails who would be my best friend and we'd make each other friendship bracelets, have sleepovers, and all that fun stuff.

But then my fantasy was crushed when I found out that my new eight year old neighbor was a boy. And not just a boy. A boy in a wheelchair.

His name was Jason and I saw him a few times from afar. He went to a different school than I did, and there was a special school bus that picked him up. I saw him waiting with his parents at the curb for the special bus, which was about half the length of the bus that picked me up. My parents told me it was a bus for disabled kids. When it arrived, a ramp would be lowered mechanically and Jason would wheel into it, and the driver would help him get arranged in the bus. My mother yelled at me not to stare, but how could I not stare?

When the Foxes had been living next door for a few weeks, we came over for a visit and to bring them a welcome basket.

My little sister Lydia and I were dressed up in uncomfortable pink clothes, and I was firmly instructed to play with Jason. Lydia, who was only four, was totally off the hook since the older Fox child was a 13 year old boy.

"I don't want to play with Jason," I whined, as my mother did up the buttons on my dress. "He's weird."

"Oh, stop it," my mother said. "He's not weird."

"He's in a wheelchair," I pointed out.

"Don't you dare mention that," my mother snapped.

"Why not?" spoke up my Nana, who was listening in. "I'm sure the boy knows he's in a wheelchair. It's not a secret, is it?"

Despite everything, I giggled. I wished my mother would let Nana come along, but they were too worried about her making a comment like that. Apparently, she lost her self-censor somewhat as she got older, although Daddy said she'd always kind of been like that.

Fifteen minutes later, my mother was shoving Lydia and me in the direction of the house next door. We rang the bell and Mrs. Fox answered, greeting us warmly. "Jill!" she cried. "I'm so glad you could make it."

"This is for you," my mother said, handing over the basket of fruit and muffins. "You met my husband, Gerald. And these are my daughters, Lydia and Tasha."

"Nice to meet you, girls," Mrs. Fox said. "My older son Randy isn't here now, but Jason is very excited to meet you."

My eyes met those of the boy sitting in a small, simple wheelchair several yards behind his mother. I could tell by his khaki slacks and lame sweater-vest that he too had been forced to dress up for the occasion. He looked just as miserable as I did.

"He's eight, isn't he?" Mom asked. "Tasha is eight as well."

"Yes, that's wonderful," Mrs. Fox said. "They could play together." She lowered her voice to a stage whisper that people a mile away could hear loud and clear: "Jason hasn't been having an easy time making new friends."

Yeah. What a shock.

With that sentiment, Jason and I were herded off in the direction of his bedroom, presumably for me to be his new best friend. We both went, sort of like lambs being led to the slaughter.

Once we were alone in Jason's room, we both just sat there awkwardly, not saying anything to each other. We were too young to even know how to make polite conversation.

I tried not to stare at Jason, but it was hard not to. I mean, really hard. Why did he need a wheelchair anyway? Maybe he had some awful disease where he was dying. Maybe it was contagious! Maybe he had some contagious fatal disease and my mother had locked me alone in a room with him. She'd be so sorry when I died.

Although to be honest, Jason didn't really look like he was dying. He looked pretty much like a normal kid, but he was sitting in a wheelchair. He had short brown hair that it looked like his mother had attempted to comb yet he'd managed to get it messy again before our arrival. He had green eyes that were bright, even in spite of how clearly miserable he was at the moment. And then there were the freckles that were sprinkled down either side of his nose, although those disappeared years later.

I was perched gingerly on Jason's bed. He had Star Wars blankets. Actually, I had to admit, he had some pretty cool toys.

My mother always bought me dolls, but the thing is, dolls didn't do much. Maybe these days, dolls cry and piss their diapers or whatever, but back then, in the eighties, dolls were much less interesting. But Jason had toys that did cool stuff. He had toy cars and trucks, he had a rocket, and a huge box of Legos. But what really piqued my interest was that he had what looked like a huge box of TRANSFORMERS.

Confession time: I loved Transformers. I watched the TV show religiously every Saturday, rooting for the Autobots to defeat the evil Decepticons. But nobody would buy me any Transformers because I was a girl and obviously it's not an appropriate toy for girls. So I had about half a dozen My Little Ponies and at least a dozen Barbie dolls, but no cars that turned into robots. It was a source of frustration for me. Every time I asked my mother, she'd say, "What do you want one of those awful toys for? You're a girl!"

But Jason, he owned the mother lode.

"Um," I said, working up my nerve. "Are those, um, Transformers?"

Jason brightened. "Yeah. You like Transformers?"

I nodded shyly.

To my delight, Jason grabbed the whole big box and dumped them out on his bed. He seriously had every Transformer in existence. He had Optimus Prime, of course, most of the Autobots, Megatron, the Decepticons including the cassette spies, plus a bunch of the newer ones like the Dinobots, the Insecticons, and even

Devastator. I was majorly impressed. If I were a little older, I would have creamed myself or something.

"Oh my god," I breathed. "You're the luckiest person alive."